Trinity's Daughter

Trinity's Daughter

Betty Byrd

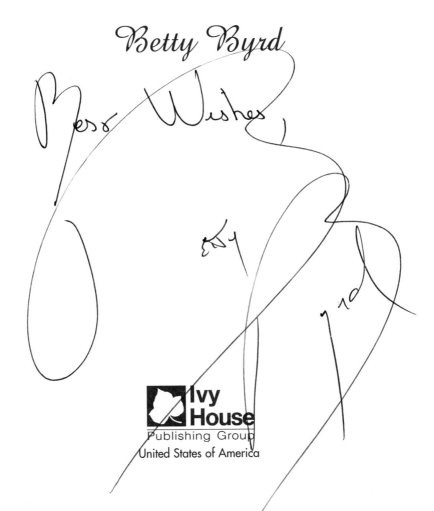

Ivy House
Publishing Group
United States of America

PUBLISHED BY IVY HOUSE PUBLISHING GROUP
5122 Bur Oak Circle, Raleigh, NC 27612
United States of America
919-782-0281

ISBN: 1-57197-313-3
Library of Congress Control Number: 2001 135836

Printed in the United States of America

For Bill, Lizz and Kortnee

TABLE OF CONTENTS

PART I
Brya Fitzgibbons

PART II
Olivia Hunter

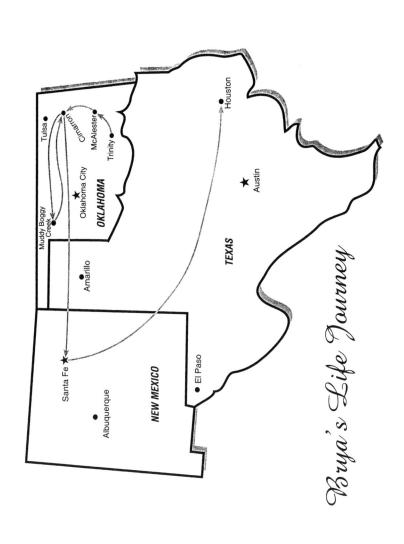

Brya's Life Journey

"Family faces are magic mirrors.
Looking at people who belong
to us, we see the past, present
and future."
—*Gail Lumet Buckley*

ACKNOWLEDGMENTS

Writing a novel is a long journey. Along the path you encounter individuals who keep you focused on the finish line.

Abundant gratitude goes out to my long time friend, author and copy editor, Lynette Triere. Your encouragement, perception and quiet wisdom kept me fortified. Thank you for being there every step of the way.

To Kay Garrett, my line editor, who taught me what writing was all about. Thank you for making me jump the hurdle.

Hats off to Peggy Villines and Anne Reilly for believing in this story and pushing me to write it.

Thank you to Lita Arvizu, my right hand. Your positive attitude and humor propelled me every inch of the way.

To Christopher Walsh, Clinical Director at Casa de Amparo, your expertise on abused children and families lit my path.

To my cheering section of family and friends, your patience and keen interest kept me going.

And finally, to Carol MacIntire, my best friend from high school who died of breast cancer, thank you for always believing that I had talent. I crossed the finish line for you.

To my readers, thank you for taking this journey with me.

PART I: *Brya Fitzgibbons*

Weathering the Depression

Black Tuesday, October 29, 1929

"Careful now," Beatrice Fitzgibbons said. The children spilled out of the doorway, past the columns and steps, broad-jumping their way to freedom. Beatrice sat in her rocking chair, fanning herself with a magnolia leaf. The day was hot. Her hair lay moist on her neck. She tried to adjust one of her corset stays—which held up her ample bosom—but she couldn't get comfortable.

She enjoyed watching her children play, and in case they hurt themselves, she was there. She fiddled with them whenever they came near, adjusting their collars, straightening their dresses and combing back their hair. Beatrice focused her gaze on the expansive lawn and her five offspring: Brya, sixteen; Brock, seventeen; Duke, twelve; Megan, thirteen; and Emilia, fifteen. Her favorite was Brya, to whom she could never say no.

"That stupid Brock stole my new straw hat, Mama," Brya yelled.

"What did you do to your brother that made him take your hat? You ought to know by now that if you tease him, he'll tease you back."

"I didn't do nothing, Mama."

Beatrice looked at Brya like she always did in situations like this.

"You're one sassy child, Brya Fitzgibbons. You have a hankering for mischief, which shows in those turquoise eyes of yours. No one needs to tell you how to get what you want. Tell your brother I said he should give your hat back, right now."

"Yes, Mama."

Brya tossed her long white hair and skipped off into the grass toward one of the giant magnolia trees.

"Emilia, what are you doing?"

"Duke and I are playing gin rummy. Want to play?"

"No thanks, I'm trying to find my hat that Brock stole."

Emilia swatted a fly off her nose and looked up. "Go and find that brother of ours. He's always pulling some prank."

Emilia was fifteen years old with auburn hair that hung like a curtain to her waist. Duke, the youngest, was twelve, going on two. And Megan, thirteen, never left Beatrice's side; in fact, she was sitting at her side now, keeping her company. She would grow up just like her mother. Brock was the spitting image of his father, John Fitzgibbons Jr.; both were handsome—built broad with curly black hair and penetrating dark eyes.

As Brya scoured the grounds of the plantation house, a sudden breeze blew, and the scent of magnolia and honey-suckle filled the air. The crickets were busy chirping out a song. Indian summer had brought an assortment of weather and moods.

After combing the strawberry patch for her hat, Brya peeked over a nearby trellis and stared at Mama Beatrice.

"Mama, what's wrong?"

"Nothing to concern yourself with, child. I'm just worried about your daddy. He doesn't seem himself lately."

"I know, Mama, he really works hard. After I find my hat, I'll run to the garage to make sure he's all right."

Beatrice waved Brya on with her handkerchief and lay back in her chair, fanning herself. She couldn't remember the last time she and her husband had disappeared into their bedroom in the late afternoon. Sadness swept over her. So many memories.

❦

When John Jr. married Beatrice in her hometown of Cimarron, it was still Indian Territory. That was 1895. They lived there until John's business brought them to Trinity. Fifteen years later, they built a Georgia-style plantation home which sat on the west fork of the Trinity River. The one and a half acres was a remnant, granted by Governor W. T. Keyes in 1847 to John's father, John Sr.

John Jr. had a bridge built across the river to move the oak timbers for the construction of his house. It was common knowledge that some crooked politicians allocated the funds for this endeavor. The Fitzgibbons called their mansion the Great House because it was bigger than most houses around these parts. It had twenty-one rooms, fifteen bathrooms, and cost two hundred thousand dollars to build.

The entrance to the Great House was flanked by magnolias and black, wrought iron gates. White pillars sat on red-tiled porches. The house wrapped around the end of the street like a snake. Since Beatrice was frail and too much heat gave her sunstroke, John Jr. had a cover built over the porch which provided coolness and shade.

❦

Brya pushed open the mahogany front door, and became entertained by the colors of the stained glass. Where is that hat? she thought. Dark wood enveloped the stairways, ceilings, and floors. In the winter, fireplaces provided heat for every room in the house. At the back of the entrance hall, Brya feverishly went through the music room where Emilia,

3

a budding concert pianist, would practice her piano. She even delved into the piano bench praying that her hat was hidden there. But it wasn't. She flew into the library, tossing satin pillows on the floor, and searching under cushions. She laughed, recalling how Brock and Duke were made to spend hours there, reading to improve their minds.

It didn't take long before she reached her favorite place—Beatrice's bathroom. Here, she was surrounded by mirrors, lavender soaps, and lotions. Brya liked to admire herself in her mama's clothes, and pretend she was a princess. She stopped to stare into the mirror over the sink. Her hair looked messy, so she opened one of the treasure-filled drawers to pick out one of Beatrice's boar-bristle hairbrushes. She brushed her hair, sweeping it up to the side, pretending for a moment that she was the princess of the household.

"Enough of this," she said out loud. "I have to catch that Brock." Brya raced down the steps and out the front door. Beatrice was still fanning herself, staring out at the perfect lawn and her active brood.

Eusabia, the Negro housekeeper, appeared carrying a small, silver tray with a cookie and a drink on it. "Excuse me, Miz Fitzgibbons, would you care for some fresh lemonade? It's a mighty hot day out here." Eusabia mopped the sweat from the sides of her full face.

"Yes, Eusabia, that will be grand. Please bring plenty for the children, too."

"Yes um." Eusabia headed back to her kitchen.

"Mama, what do you think about when you sit here?" Brya asked, sitting down at her feet to rest. Megan reluctantly moved over.

"Today I've just been thinking about the wonderful life your daddy has given us, when others have nothing. People think of him as dedicated, attentive, loving, and respectful. But I'm worried. Lately, he's been keeping to himself."

Beatrice looked away and wiped her eyes.

"What does Daddy do?" Brya asked.

Beatrice sniffed and mustered a tiny smile. "Your daddy handles thousands and thousands of head of cattle that he keeps at six ranches throughout the country. He also owns oil wells. More than we can count. And he built the first bank in town, the First Western Bank of Trinity, Oklahoma."

"Maybe Daddy will let me drill an oil well someday," Brya said.

"Women don't do those things, honey," Beatrice replied. "You just learn to attend to the needs of your husband."

Beatrice's job was to chaperone the children. She wasn't interested in business. Most women weren't. John handled all that. She was best at having parties, and no one gave a party quite like her. The decorations were impressive, and her gentle and kind nature graced all who attended.

Mama Beatrice stopped fanning herself for a moment and picked up the folded newspaper from the side table. The headline read: *STOCK MARKET CRASHES—BANKS CLOSE!*

"What? John said that stocks had doubled over the last five years. Surely this doesn't affect us!" Beatrice gazed up at the limestone columns. They made her feel safe and secure.

"Mama, what's wrong?"

"Never mind my outburst, Brya. When your daddy comes in for dinner he'll tell us that we don't have a thing to worry about."

Eusabia waddled out on the porch with more icy glasses of lemonade, and fresh oatmeal-raisin cookies. She liked to surprise the family with special treats. The children came swarming to the cool porch like bees to honey. The chilled lemonade felt soothing on their parched throats.

"Once you've finished your drinks and cookies," Beatrice announced, "go into the house. You've been out in the heat too . . ."

Before she finished her words, Emilia, Duke, Megan, and Brock, having gobbled down their treats, ran past her, pushing and shoving each other into the house and up the winding staircase.

"Brock, give me my hat before you go into your room," demanded Brya.

"I can't hear you!" her brother called down.

Eusabia placed the crystal glasses on a tray. Brya handed her a pink rosebud china plate she was about to leave behind.

Beatrice stood up and stretched.

"Thank you, Mama," Brya said. "I'm headed to the garage to find Daddy. I'll be back in a minute." She blew her a kiss.

Beatrice smiled and nodded, and proceeded to plop herself down into her rocking chair. Her daughter would get John to come in.

Brya ran toward the garage, fighting off the pink mimosa blossoms that flew in her face. She was hellbent on finding her hat, once again, and her daddy.

As she rounded the back side of the house, Brya called out, "Daddy! Where are you?" Nothing.

She saw traces of sunlight bouncing off the rear end of her family's black Model T Ford. She was almost to the garage and yelled once again, "Daddy!" But it was still quiet.

As she darted through the garage door, she stopped in her tracks. There, facing her, sat her great and gentle daddy with a shotgun under his chin. His eyes were looking right past her. "Daddy!! No!!" she screamed. "Don't . . ." But before Brya could finish, he fired a shot through his head, scattering his brains everywhere.

Brya screamed hysterically, trying to brush his blood and gray jellied insides off her dress, but the more she tried, the more it smeared.

Suddenly, her head was reeling and she saw nothing but white. When she came to, she found herself draped over his lifeless body, never to forget the smell of warm blood pouring out of him.

She slowly lifted her face off of her daddy's chest and looked up to see Mama Beatrice staring down at them. Her face was lifeless.

"Mama! Mama! Daddy's dead! I saw him put a gun to his head. I saw him die! I saw it."

Beatrice's eyes stayed fixed on her husband. She didn't speak. Then suddenly, she wailed, and crumbled onto his body.

"Mama, get up! Mama, talk to me!" Brya shook her as hard as she could, then held her mama's face in her trembling hands. Brya tried to get her mama to look at her, but Beatrice's eyes saw something else.

"Mama, don't you leave, too. Not now! I need you!" Brya shouted.

She ran out of the barn and screamed, "Eusabia, Eusabia!"

Eusabia, who had been cleaning the porch, heard Brya's frantic cry. She came dashing across the front lawn and saw Brya running toward her, red from head to toe.

"Lawdie child, yuz covered with blood! What's happened?"

"Eusabia!" Brya fell hard into her soft body. "Daddy shot himself in the head, and now Mama won't answer me."

Eusabia looked up at the sky and prayed, "Oh dear Lawd in heaven, have mercy on us!" She stroked Brya's head. "Tell me, tell me, Lawd, that this ain't happening to this fine family!" Eusabia took a deep breath, and cradled

Brya's face in her hands. "Go into the house and call the sheriff. I'll tend to your mama and papa."

"No! No, Eusabia," Brya yelled. "Don't leave me alone. I want to go with you!"

Eusabia placed her hands on Brya's shoulders, and looked her straight in the eye. "No, child, you can't go back in there. You must never look upon that scene again."

And Brya did not.

Later that evening, Duke, Brock, Emilia, Megan and Brya were left standing in the dark on the steps of the Great House while the undertaker transported their daddy's body away to Chamberlin's Mortuary. They felt sick and terribly alone.

Brya had only known her daddy for sixteen years, but her heart and soul left with him then. She watched in silence as they drove him away.

One week later, Beatrice was taken to Greenwood Sanitarium, where she died. And the life that family had always known disappeared.

The Aftermath

It rained for days after Beatrice died. It was difficult for Brya to sleep so she was always the first one up, each day, after Eusabia.

One morning Brya sat down for breakfast and read the headline in the newspaper: *BANKS FAIL ACROSS THE NATION: The Cancerous Hands of the Great Depression Continue to Spread their Deadly Fingers Across the United States and the World*. Eusabia brought in smoked bacon, hot biscuits, and cocoa.

"Eusabia, what does 'cancerous' mean?"

"Oh Lawdie, child, it's that ravenous sickness that took my sister. What on earth makes you ask?"

Brya pointed to the headline, smearing bacon grease on the page. "And what's this Great Depression, anyway?"

"I don't knowz a whole lot, Brya. What I does know is folks have lost their homes and theyz got no money."

"Is that why my daddy shot himself?"

With tears welling up in her eyes, Eusabia hesitated, "Yes, child. God rest his soul. Enough of this talk. Finish some of this here bacon and I'll make you some fried eggs."

The Fitzgibbons children were no exception to the Depression. The Great House was going to be sold. What would the world outside their gates be like? Frightened and sad, they whispered amongst themselves constantly.

After the funeral, Charles, one of John Jr.'s older brothers from Kansas City, and his wife, Kate, were to stay behind until the Great House sold, and the decisions made about where the children would live. Uncle Charles and Aunt Kate adored their kin and enjoyed taking care of them since they were not able to have a family of their own.

❧

The Great House sold in a matter of days for twenty thousand dollars cash, to Mr. E. R. Bennett, owner of the *Trinity Star Telegram*. The children were given five hundred dollars and one piece of furniture each to help start them in their new lives. Relatives would soon come to take them away.

All of Beatrice's french furniture, oriental rugs, silver, china, and precious art objects were taken to a private auction house. The money from the sale would pay for their father's funeral, the sanitarium, the auction house, and Eusabia. What little money was left would feed the family until everyone was gone.

The president of the First Western Bank held a fire sale on the cattle ranches and the oil wells—all for personal gain. Everything was lost.

With the house almost empty, Brya had nothing left to hang on to but her brothers and sisters. She didn't know when she would see them again.

Their last night together would remain burned in Brya's memory forever. Black Tuesday had come and gone, but the Depression was getting worse.

It was a cold and rainy evening in early November. Indian summer had not lasted long and it looked like winter would come earlier than usual. Brya planned a slumber party in her daddy's study. She wanted to make sure that none of her brothers and sisters would be alone on the last night.

Brock and Duke gathered firewood from the shed to make a fire. Brya watched as they brought the wood in through the back door and walked through the empty halls of the Great House. She could hear nothing but the echoes of their footsteps. Each child clung to the one piece of furniture that belonged to them. Now, with those few furnishings and a warm fire, Emilia, Megan, Duke, Brock, and Brya would pretend that this had all been a bad dream.

They listened to Uncle Charles and Aunt Kate upstairs, talking, just like their parents used to do. Eusabia was still in her kitchen cooking food for each of them to take on their journey. The grandfather clock that had lulled them to sleep on many an evening, chimed that the end of the day was near.

Brya chose to keep her mama's daybed. It was almost as wide as a regular bed, with carved swans' heads on either end. The upholstery was brown and pink french tapestry—Beatrice's favorite. The daybed held many memories for Brya. Beatrice laid motionless on the bed before they took her away. Brya's parents had spent their wedding night on it, and whenever she was feverish, Beatrice let her rest there. Brya swore never to let it go because she needed something to keep with her to remember her parents by.

She sat on the bed and stared at the fire, pulling her knees into her belly. She drew the comforter up to her chin.

"Brock, are you still going to follow your dream to be a big oil man?" Brya asked.

"I sure am. But as you already know, first I have to live with Charles and Kate, and then on to a military academy there in Kansas City for a few years. But after graduation, I'm leaving for South America to work as a roughneck in the oil fields."

"Oh, Brock! Will I ever see you again?" She threw off her comforter and ran to hug her brother—so tight that he couldn't catch his breath.

"Aww, sure sis, you'll hear from me. I'm going to make lots of money in the oil business, and then I'm headed back here to live. I'll make this town respect our name again!" Brock sat down confidently in his daddy's favorite leather chair. The boy used to sit there and pretend he was a big oil man. It was only fitting that he should have it.

Brya's sister Emilia was sitting on her piano bench next to the concert Steinway. She stood up and announced, "After I go to Uncle William's house, maybe we can visit each other by train. Dallas can't be too far away. Of course, I'll have to wait until after I've finished my studies with Paderewski. He'll be teaching there only for part of next year. I plan to be a great composer and concert pianist and make Mama and Daddy proud of me."

"You'll be terrific," Brock said. "If anyone can do it, you can!"

"Why, Brock? You've never been that nice to me. What's gotten into you?"

"I may have teased you all these years, but I always knew you had it in you to be famous."

With that, Emilia cried and threw her arms around Brock. "No need to get so gushy," he said. Everyone laughed.

"Duke, you haven't told us about your plans," Megan said. He looked lost and alone, staring into the fire as the orange flames danced their final dance.

"Dad's cousin Nina, in Mississippi, is supposed to be really nice, but I don't want to stay there. I don't really know what I'm planning to do. Maybe I'll join Brock in South America." Duke was on Beatrice's favorite sofa, his hands cradling his head while one leg was draped over the arm.

"We're never going to see each other again!" Megan cried out.

"Megan," Duke replied, "stop all this sobbing and moaning, for God's sake. We've already talked about all this. Of course we'll be together some day—we're family! Anyways, are you still going to live on some farm in Oklahoma City?"

"Yes, with Daddy's brother and his wife Claire," said Megan. "Aunt Kate says that Auntie Claire has lots of animals for me to take care of, and I'll have my own room."

"Megan, remember that Oklahoma City's not too far from where I'll be in Cimarron," Brya added. "I'm sure that Grandpa Patch and Grandma Eugenia will help me get to your house, so we can visit. So you see, we're going to be just fine."

"The newspaper's been talking about all the children living in train yards and camps called 'hobo jungles,'" Brock added. "And it makes me realize one thing—no matter what happens to us, we still don't have it half as bad as some of those people."

Emilia lit some candles and sat them on either side of the black, baby grand piano. They each said their last goodnight, and promised that they would all get together as soon as they could find a way. Emilia lulled everyone to sleep, except Brya, with one of Beethoven's sonatas. After the last note was played, and the fire had drawn its last breath, Brya motioned for Emilia to crawl in their mother's bed with her.

"I love you, sis."

"I love you too, Brya. Don't ever forget me."

They cried themselves to sleep.

The next morning was almost as black as the night before. All five children stood in front of the large bay window watching the rain run down the glass. To them, it seemed as though the window was weeping. It didn't feel like a day to leave but more like a day to sit by the fire and drink hot chocolate. But that luxury was no longer theirs.

Breakfast smelled especially good that morning as Eusabia brought in some steaming porridge. She had promised the children she would stay at the Great House until all of them had gone.

"Eusabia," Brya asked, "what are you going to do with yourself after we leave?"

"Oh, child," she said, handing Brya a bowl of porridge. "I've always had a good-luck angel that sits here on my shoulder." She patted herself. "So don't you worry, he'll take good care of me. He's sittin' on your shoulder, too. You just reach up an' give him a pat every now an' then."

All the children reached up and touched the top of their shoulders. Brya looked into the soft doe eyes of her ever-faithful Eusabia and gave her a big hug. This was the last time she would feel the soft, warm body that had been there for her so many times before. Brya didn't want to let go.

"Eusabia, I'm going to take my angel with me and maybe one day I can have a family, live in a grand house, and you can come and take care of all of us. If the angel grants me that wish, then I'll never, ever leave my family, no matter what happens!" Brya smiled at Eusabia while trying to hold back her tears. She didn't want to cry anymore.

Eusabia took charge.

"Now, all of you chillen get your clothes put on. Mr. Charles says that y'all be picked up before noon. Your kinfolks will be here an' they'll take you home with them. No cryin' either when you leave! There's been enough of that. You has to go on and be strong!"

Eusabia hugged each of them, then picked up the empty porridge bowls. As she left the room, Brya watched her wipe her eyes with her apron.

Brya was to be the first to leave. Since most of her belongings were sold at the auction, she didn't have much to take. Brya carefully packed some of her clothes and her personal items in two suitcases and placed them on top of the daybed next to the front door. Everything that she owned was sitting in the foyer.

Suddenly she heard a loud honk and opened the front door to see who had arrived. There, parked out in front, was a black Ford pickup truck with a dirty canvas top. Brya had seen pictures of one in a magazine but never the actual thing.

"Aunt Kate, Uncle Charles, Eusabia, someone's here!" Brya called out. "Come quickly!" Everyone came running down the empty hall and peered outside.

"Brya," Aunt Kate said, "it's your grandfather, Patch Gilmore. Come with me, child."

For years, Patch and Eugenia had disapproved of John's unscrupulous associates and business dealings. For the sake of the grandchildren and Beatrice, their visits had been limited.

Brya couldn't take her eyes off of the distinguished gentleman who was walking up the steps, and also—now that she was going to live with him—saw him in a whole new light.

Aunt Kate said hello and gave him a hug. His opened umbrella had not covered his back, and he was drenched from the long walk up to the porch.

"How's your husband doing, Kate?"

"Why, he's fine. Everything is just fine."

It seemed that no matter what happened to anyone in the South, everything was always just fine. That was how Aunt Kate acted while she brushed the drops of water off his coat.

"How are you doing, Patch?"

"I'm doing as well as can be expected."

Grandpa Patch glanced around at all the eyes that were on him.

"I'm so sorry that I didn't visit Beatrice the week she was at the sanitarium. We had just returned home from John's funeral, and when I heard she had been placed in the sanitarium, her mother and I were making plans to come and stay for a while, to help. I thought she would eventually pull out of it." Grandpa Patch hung his head. "I've just spent a long while at her grave, wondering why all this has happened." He pulled out a crumpled handkerchief from his back pocket and wiped his tears. Kate put her arms around him. "I swear, Kate, even though our differences with John didn't make it possible to visit Beatrice very often, her death makes all of that bickering seem so senseless." Brya watched as her grandfather pulled himself together and looked over Aunt Kate's shoulder and down into her eyes. "You must be Brya?" he asked in a very different voice.

"Yes, sir, I am," Brya replied shyly. She had forgotten how slow her grandpa talked. Actually, it was soothing.

"You look just like your mother did when she was your age. Did anyone ever tell you that you have the most beautiful eyes, my child?"

"Yes, sir, they have." Her answer made him grin. He put his large hand out to greet her small one. She slipped inside his strong grip and immediately felt secure. Grandpa Patch looked around. "Well, I haven't seen all of you children as often as I would have liked. Between your Grandma Eugenia's gout and your daddy's desire to have it all, there weren't many opportunities." Patch stopped himself. He had too many mixed emotions about John Jr. This was not the place to lash out. He cleared his throat. "You're a fine looking family. You do your parents proud."

"Miss Brya, I've been told that we are to take your mama's daybed with us," Grandpa Patch said.

Brya nodded.

"I borrowed a friend's truck so that you can bring it back with you. We'll need the help of your family to lift it in."

Brya nodded again.

Everyone rallied around the daybed, covering it with an old piece of canvas so that it wouldn't get ruined by the rain. Brock and Duke wanted to be in charge of the hoist. Their lean, muscled arms lifted it into the back of the truck, and Brya watched as they tied it down with rope. Everyone made sure that the elaborate piece of furniture would not be affected by the elements before it reached Cimarron.

Patch and Brya were now ready to leave. Even though many tears had been shed the night before, Brya's eyes began to spill over once again. She felt empty and alone. There was a hard lump in her stomach, and another in her throat. She was scared to death.

Patch placed his hand underneath Brya's elbow to guide her gently through the sad gathering. Emilia handed her a song that she had written especially for her sister. Next, Brock slipped a wet envelope full of Fitzgibbons soil in her hand. Megan took off her gold locket and chain and placed it around Brya's neck. Duke promised that he would always be there for her, no matter what happened, but Brya knew she could never count on him because he had always been unreliable.

Brya gave everyone a kiss and promised to write regularly. Eusabia brought out a picnic basket with plenty of food to last on their journey. Everyone lined up once again, to wave good-bye.

As Brya climbed up into the truck, wiping the rain off her face, she gazed at the Great House and knew that it would be far too painful to ever visit this place again.

Patch started the engine and began to move toward the gates. Brya's right hand never stopped waving until the Great House, her brothers and sisters, Eusabia, Aunt Kate, and Uncle Charles become nothing more than memories stranded on the horizon.

❦

"Grandpa Patch," Brya asked, looking out the window of the truck, "can we cross over the Trinity River one more time before I go?"

"Brya, you've read my mind. That's exactly the way we're headed in order to catch Highway 33." Patch looked at her and smiled. "In fact, we're almost there now."

Brya looked out the left side of the truck and saw the beginning of her river, where she had shared many happy picnics with her family. She remembered telling the river that it belonged only to her, and nobody else could have it. When she was a baby, she was baptized there. Her daddy was the one who held her. His strong arms always surrounded her like a blanket. She realized that her soul belonged to her daddy and the Trinity. Brya started to cry and rolled down her window to savor the last smell. Once they crossed over the bridge, she would lose sight of it. Brya turned away and closed her eyes as they crossed over, and said a silent farewell. This great river, with its deep channel and steep, grassy banks, would always remain in her heart.

Brya opened her locket. How ironic—a picture of her and Megan—together forever.

"Now that we've crossed the Trinity," Patch said, "I plan on heading north until we reach our destination. We have about two hundred and fifty miles to travel, Brya—about two days."

She had never been in a car that long in her life, let alone a truck. "Where are we going to stay tonight?" she asked, staring down the lonely road.

"Since it's so desolate, I thought we'd camp by the side of the road. When I drove to pick you up, I saw lots of road camps. Folks have lost so much in this depression that they are homeless, so they're migrating to other places in the country. We'll just have to see what develops."

Brya was afraid because she had never before slept around people she didn't know. She turned in her seat and stared at her grandpa. She wanted to trust him. He looked trustworthy, and had a strong and steady voice. He was tall and lean, and what little gray hair he had, he combed to the side. She thought that he must use pomade on his hair because it never moved a lick. Brya decided that she wanted to know more about this man who was taking her to stay with migrants.

"Grandpa Patch, what's your life been like?"

Patch adjusted himself in his seat and replied, "Well, I've done a lot of things. I was born in Charles County, Missouri. When I was eighteen, I left for the hill country of Texas, near Austin, where I got a job as a farm hand. It paid me twelve dollars and fifty cents a month. Two months later, I was offered a job on a ranch, where I helped drive cattle over the old Chisholm Trail. We had about twenty five hundred head on my first drive to Colorado. The trick was to get the cattle there and back home, all in the same year."

Brya's eyes widened as she became captivated by her grandpa's tale. He continued. "Finally, I decided to settle down. I met and married your Grandma Eugenia. Your mama, Beatrice, was born right away. We started a little ranch by the Pecos River, and a few years later the town of Pecos sprang up. Four years after that, I sold our ranch, and Eugenia and I moved to Cimarron, Oklahoma. Your grandma gave birth to a son, Josh, who died shortly thereafter of pneumonia. Your mama was all we had. In 1893, Cimarron was in the process of being changed from Twin Territories, Indian and Oklahoma, to just the Oklahoma

Territory, and we didn't have much of a town. Josh was only the third person to be buried in the cemetery."

Brya wanted to feel sorry for him but he had a way of making sure that you didn't.

"I'm sorry you lost your little boy," Brya said sadly. "And now you've lost your daughter, too. My mama."

Patch nodded. Brya didn't say a whole lot but when she spoke, it was the right thing to be said at the time. Beatrice had taught her that.

"Well, Brya, I stayed a cattleman for about fourteen years. Would you believe that I helped start the First Bank of Cimarron, and we are one of the few banks that's still open? I suppose we're mighty lucky. We aren't rich people, never have been, but we never needed to live big and that's paid off. As president of the bank, I'm very concerned about the current situation."

"What's happened, Grandpa?"

"The farmers lost their crops because it hasn't rained in Oklahoma for a long time. This made the topsoil so dry that the area we'll be driving through is full of wind-driven dust storms. Sadly enough, farmers have been forced off their land to find other work. But there is none."

"Did Daddy lose his job?"

Patch swallowed and hesitated. "Yes, honey, your daddy lost his job. Now, why don't you rest and I'll tell you more later." He patted Brya on the head, just like her mama used to do, and continued to drive.

She laid her head against the cool, glass window. The man she thought was going to be a stern and unfriendly grandpa had turned out to be a safe and gentle man. That was the last thing she remembered.

❦

Brya slept a good four hours. When she woke up, and rubbed the sand out of her eyes, she couldn't believe what she was seeing—a sign that read Highway 66 and a line of ragged travelers with haunted looks on their faces. They were walking on the side of the highway, some alone, some in groups. Patch had joined a large caravan of broken-down trucks, a few with overheating engines, all just chugging along. There was no sign of rain, just flat land for as far as the eye could see, with dirt blowing in the wind. Families were pulling everything they owned behind them in small carts and children's red wagons. The migrants' bodies looked sun-dried and windburned. Everything was parched.

It looked like the end of the world.

"Oh, Grandpa, what's happened to these people?" Brya said as she rubbed the goosebumps on her arms and stared out at the forlorn faces.

"This, my sweet girl, is the result of our times. These are the folks I was telling you about. They've lost everything."

A few people were camped by the side of the road cooking what looked like stew in dirty pots. Others laid on the parched earth, weak and dying. Feeling sick to her stomach, Brya rolled down her window only to be struck by the smell of sweat, dust, and decay.

"Grandpa, I don't feel so well." She bent over and clutched her stomach.

"I'm sorry that you have to see this despair. The Depression is destroying thousands of families, and you're seeing the worst of it right here in Oklahoma."

Brya reached into the picnic basket for a jar of lemonade, and began sipping on it. Their truck stopped for a moment to let an old man cross the road. His trousers were so torn that there were no knees in them and his hands were black. He seemed bewildered, unsure of where he was going. As Brya put the bottle to her lips, she glanced outside. A young girl about her age, all skin and bones, was standing there looking at her. The girl's face was like a leather mask stretched over bone, and her hollow, blue eyes were squinting to avoid the bright afternoon sun. Dirt was caked underneath her fingernails and her faded green cotton dress was tattered and dirty. Brya felt sorry for her, and handed the jar of lemonade out the window. With her dirty hands, the girl reached out and grabbed it. She nodded her head, and drank the yellow liquid down as fast as she could. The two of them locked eyes just as Patch accelerated. From that moment on, Brya would always have a fear of being hungry and thirsty.

Patch had hopes of finding a cabin for the evening, but there were none available. It was getting dark. Although his eyes were weary by the time they reached the town of McAlester, he kept up his search for a place where they might camp for the evening. They had Eusabia's food to share, so maybe they would be welcome.

Patch stopped the truck in front of some shacks—the best of the worst they had seen. The unsecured wood on some of the rooftops was flapping in the breeze; there were lots of families living in whatever they could put together. He decided to ask if they could stay with one of them. Patch had a sincere way about him. He told Brya not to worry. If he thought for one minute that they were in danger, they'd leave.

Patch was met by two ragged little boys carrying kerosene lamps.

"Howdy, mister," they said. Their trousers were streaked with dirt.

"Howdy, yourselves," Patch replied. "May I speak to your ma or pa?" The boys hesitated for a moment, then ran into the shack. Brya noticed that her grandpa looked nervous.

Out came a middle-aged woman with cold eyes and a hard face. "What you want, mister?" She crossed her tan arms over her bony chest while looking them up and down. She looked rough, nothing like Brya's soft Mama Beatrice.

"My granddaughter and I have traveled a long distance, and we wonder if we might be able to camp with you for the evening? We have food to share and won't be any bother. As soon as the sun comes up we'll be on our way."

The woman called her husband out of the shack. He walked with a limp. His brown hair stood straight up, and his cotton trousers were hanging low on his body, leaving his long underwear hanging out the top. It looked like he grabbed them a lot because there were greasy handprints around the waist. What was left of his teeth were stained dark brown. Brya had never seen a man like this and she crouched down in the truck, shivering.

The husband took a good look at Patch's truck and then a longer look at Patch. "Well, I reckon you can stay, but we got no extra blankets. You'll have to sleep wherever you can find room."

"That's fine. You're kind to let us stay," Patch said as he headed back to the truck to get Brya, and Eusabia's food.

Patch held his granddaughter's trembling hand as they walked toward the rickety lean-to.

"What's your name, ma'am?" Patch asked as he laid the picnic basket by the fire.

"Folks call me Ernestine, and this here's my husband, Frank. These are our two boys, Luke and Jake. Who are you?"

Patch put his arm around Brya's shoulder. "This is my granddaughter, Brya, and I'm Patch Gilmore."

Ernestine bent down over the fire and began tending the steaming pot of white potato stew without saying anything more.

Patch reached into the picnic basket, and handed Ernestine a jar of homemade apricot preserves and a loaf of Eusabia's famous caraway bread. She lifted the bread to her nose and sniffed it for a long time. This perked her up a bit and she exclaimed, "Looky here everybody, we done have us some homemade bread!" This got everyone's lips smiling, and Patch and Brya were finally accepted. Brya stayed close to her grandpa though. To her, these were scary folks.

As the night fell, it got colder and colder. There were lots of critters prowling around foraging for leftover scraps. The only sounds that they heard were distant voices around nearby campfires, and the hooting of a barn owl. Brya had a warm coat on and she was grateful she'd kept it. They sat around the blazing fire and shared stories about what happened to them. Frank had been a roughneck on some Oklahoma wells until his leg was blown off in a gas explosion. When the Depression hit, they ran out of money. The only thing left to do was to pick cotton for about no pay, whenever he could find a farmer with some good land who needed help. Right now, the family didn't know where they were headed. Brya couldn't imagine this because she was headed somewhere to live. However, she could identify with losing everything that was important to her. Even though they were not from the same side of the tracks, losing was losing, no matter what you had.

After they swapped stories, it was time to go to sleep. The inside of the shack made Brya squirm. At least outside, kerosene lamps burned their bright light. The tin house inside held nothing but darkness. Dirty, stained mattresses lay wall-to-wall on the dry soil floor. Patch had some extra horse blankets that he traveled with and told Brya to roll up in one. Frightened and missing her home, she wrapped herself in the scratchy blanket and curled up in the corner. Brya fell asleep next to her grandpa while listening to the sound of the tin door trembling in the wind.

When the morning sun peered through every crack in the lean-to, they all got up. With the help of her boys, Ernestine got the fire going again while Patch and Brya offered up more bread, preserves, and beef jerky.

Afterwards, Brya was anxious to go to the bathroom. Her grandpa showed her the way to a clump of bushes nearby and told her to do her business there. She had no choice. After she squatted, almost falling over, she felt dirty and degraded because she had nothing to wipe herself with. Brya began to cry as she walked back.

Patch and Brya ate and parted ways. They waved good-bye as they clanked down the bumpy road to the highway.

"How far are we from Cimarron, Grandpa?"

"We have another few hours on the road, child." He pulled over to a gas station to fill up.

"I've got to go to the bathroom again," Brya said, gingerly crossing her legs.

"Well, young lady, go use the outhouse over there," Patch said, pointing to the side of the station.

She reached into the picnic basket and took out a monogrammed cloth napkin to wipe herself. She walked to the outhouse and did her duty, tossing the expensive cloth into the black hole. The putrid smell lingered in her nose as she gagged her way back to the car.

"By the way, where's Cimarron?" she asked, trying to forget what it had been like in there.

"We're just southeast of Tulsa." Patch placed the hose from the gas pump in the tank.

As he filled the truck, Brya was intrigued watching the honey-colored gasoline swirl up into the glass top of the pump. She'd never seen this happen before because the family chauffeur had always taken care of these things. Although offensive, the smell of gasoline was still better than the smell of that outhouse. Patch replaced the nozzle on the pump, and left for a few minutes to pay the gas station attendant. He returned with two chilled bottles of Dr. Pepper. As they drove back onto the highway, they saw buzzards circling over some dying cattle in a deserted pasture.

Brya grimaced and turned her face away from the grotesque sight. She couldn't wait to get away from here.

As the next couple of hours dragged by, Brya saw fewer and fewer shanties and shacks, and not as many folks living in their cars.

"Why are the people around here doing better than the others?" she asked.

"Well, sweetheart, some farmers didn't lose their crops, and their water wells didn't go dry. They were able to get by on what they raised. But there weren't many. I thank the Lord everyday that I'm among the few human beings who didn't suffer much." Patch took Brya's hand and gave it a strong squeeze. She squeezed him back and felt thankful, too.

"What's that town up ahead, Grandpa?"

"That's Cimarron."

Brya jumped up and down in her seat. "We're here, we're finally here."

He glanced at the watch that he always wore on the inside of his large wrist, raised his eyebrow and said, "If you can be patient for just about twenty more minutes, I'll deliver you to our front door."

She could hardly wait.

A New Start

Cimarron was not what Brya envisioned. Nothing was like what she had been used to, but Patch seemed proud to show her the sights.

"See that red brick building over there, the one with the stained glass and large white steeple on it?"

"Yes, sir," Brya said, trying to act interested.

"That's Eugenia's and my church. We're Methodists."

"Religion hasn't done me much good so far," Brya replied.

"That's no way to talk. The good Lord is on your side. One day you'll see."

As the scenery moved by, it didn't seem as beautiful or important as Trinity. There weren't ornate houses or richly dressed people here. This wasn't a place she would want to stay in forever. Brya knew that she was born to have much more than this small town could ever give her.

Patch interrupted her thoughts, "Over there's the courthouse and town hall. The citizens hold their meetings there in the afternoons, and don't use it as a courthouse much. There aren't many tricksters or crooks here except our very own Judge Teesdale. He's one slippery fella, Brya. Before he became a judge, when he just did his lawyering, you never knew whose side he was on because he made sure he got paid by everyone. Now, he's worse, and his docket isn't that full, so he regularly holds court at several of our saloons. You don't know much about Prohibition, but there are people that don't want liquor here in these United States. Our Judge doesn't really care about that and probably has his own personal bootlegger bring alcohol to his house. By the way, if you look out your window on the right side, you'll see my bank."

Brya rolled down the window and leaned her head out to look up. She couldn't help but compare the building to her daddy's. This one was much smaller.

"That's nice, Grandpa." She felt uncomfortable. Maybe she was just tired from the long journey and things would look better after a soak in the bathtub and a good night's sleep.

"Grandpa Patch, I'm worn out. Are we near your house yet?"

He turned down a nice, shady road called South Drury Lane, which had row upon row of three-story houses with pretty green lawns. They all looked the same.

"Brya, welcome to your new home. Did anyone ever tell you when this house was built?"

"No sir, the only thing my daddy told me was that it was built in Indian Territory."

"Well, I'll add a little more history for you. It was built in 1896 when Oklahoma was still divided into twin territories."

She wasn't interested and wanted out of the car. She didn't care about a history lesson after driving for two days, but Brya listened politely.

"The Indian Territories were the last remaining lands of the Five Civilized Tribes. When the white man wanted the land, a commission was formed to help dissolve the Indian Nations."

"Grandpa, what happened to the poor Indians? Where'd they go?"

"Well, this group of commissioners helped the tribes incorporate their towns and prepare for citizenship. By 1905, they felt that Oklahoma was ready to become a state."

Brya was silent, digesting what he had just said and studying for a moment the three-story, yellow wooden house in front of her. She continued to stare at the building that looked about the size of her garage at home. The only entrance to the porch was a gray flagstone walkway. The one bush in the front yard appeared lonely. She just wanted to go to her room and be alone.

Patch got out of the truck and opened Brya's door. "Come with me, child, let's find your grandma. We'll talk more about the Indians later."

Before they reached the front porch, a small, round, energetic woman with outstretched arms came waddling out the front door. She wore a printed cotton dress with a long-sleeved, brown wool sweater that hugged her chubby frame. Brya could hear her undergarments rubbing together as she walked.

"Land sakes, child, you're finally here, though I wish it were under different circumstances," Eugenia exclaimed, as she wiped some excess flour on her apron, and threw her generous arms around her granddaughter.

"Yes, ma'am." Brya gazed into her grandma's blue eyes, and immediately felt as contented as she did with Patch.

"Oh, Patch, it's like looking at Beatrice standing here on our porch, when she was Brya's age."

As Brya crossed the threshold, faint sounds of Hank Williams were coming from a radio in the parlor. Her daddy used to love to relax to the soulful sound of that man's voice. From the kitchen came the glorious aroma of meat loaf. A fresh apple pie was cooling on the window sill.

"I baked all of it especially for you, Brya," Eugenia said proudly.

"I can't wait to eat a home-cooked meal!"

Eugenia escorted her granddaughter to her bedroom. She showed her the small closet and the bathroom she'd use, then excused herself to set the table.

Brya's room was down the upstairs hall to the left, facing Drury Lane. It was nothing like her bedroom suite at the Great House. The walls of her room were covered in tan and white floral wallpaper, which made it appear larger than it was. A circular throw rug lay centered on the oak floor. The interior wall remained empty to accommodate her daybed. A Tiffany floor lamp stood in the corner, and next to it a roll-top desk which must have belonged to Mama Beatrice because her initials had been carved into the side of it. But it didn't feel to Brya as though this room would ever belong to her.

Her bathroom was not connected to her room but just down the hallway. It had a toilet, a tub, and a small sink, and was extremely clean. White towels hung on shiny brass racks. The beautiful, leaded stained-glass window reminded her of the one in the front door of the Great House, except that this one was much smaller. She took a long look at the colors bouncing off the walls and sank into a tired trance. When she gazed in the mirror over the white enameled sink, Brya's eyes looked tired, and her long hair was stringy and dirty. Right now, this room looked like the most important room in the house to her. Her thoughts drifted back to Mama Beatrice's bathroom. When Brya was allowed to use the bathtub, she would sink into the hot water that she laced with lavender bath oil. Brya still remembered the silky feeling it gave her. After a long soak, she loved playing dress-up with her sisters. In her mama's clothes, she would whirl through the Great House in satin mules, twirling strands of Mama Beatrice's long, white pearls.

Suddenly, her thoughts were interrupted by the voices of Patch and several men who sounded as though they were having some trouble carrying her daybed up the stairs.

"Brya, come here, I want you to meet some of the neighbors."

She scurried down the hall to where four men stood eager to greet her. The flooring was slick and with only her socks on, she flew into the room by accident. There, facing her, was one of the most handsome young men she had ever seen. His strong hand reached out to brace her fall. He's so . . . tall, she thought.

"Hello, you must be the beautiful Brya I've heard about. I'm Holden Hunter. This is my father, Virgil, and my uncles, Breen and Zeke."

She shook hands with all of them, noticing that the uncles looked a little like Frank, the migrant that Grandpa and she stayed with last night. She couldn't shake hands with Holden, being too embarrassed by her entrance.

Patch sat on the edge of the bed. "Honey, the Hunters live down the street. They generously offered to help carry your bed in, provided they could have a slice of your grandma's apple pie." The men nodded in agreement.

For some unknown reason, Brya felt shy around Holden. After the men headed down to the kitchen for a slice of pie, she went into the bathroom, slipped out of her travel clothes, and waited for her bath to draw. She tested the water with the tips of her fingers, smiled and slid in. That Holden had the most beautiful black, curly hair and deep brown eyes. "Oh well, what would he ever see in someone like me?" she said out loud, as she relaxed into the puffy, lavender fluff.

Later, after the men had all gone home, Eugenia called Brya down for dinner. After the meat loaf and apple pie were devoured, the three of them moved into the parlor by the radio for a little evening entertainment. Eugenia Gilmore was easygoing, generous, and polite to a fault. She moved about the room fluffing up pillows, making it comfortable for everyone, hardly ever sitting down herself. Brya laid on the floor, enthralled by the comedy show, *Fibber*

McGee and Molly. Life had been so serious lately that it was good to laugh again. At bedtime, she thanked them both for all they had done, and kissed them goodnight.

❦

No one woke Brya the next morning. Just as well, she needed to rest. However, when she smelled bacon cooking, down the stairs she flew. Eugenia greeted her with a cold glass of orange juice and a big hug, "Did you sleep well, child?"

"Yes, Grandma, I did. Where's Grandpa?"

"He's gone to the bank, dear, to catch up on his work. He'll be home by dinnertime. He thought you might enjoy walking around today and getting acquainted with your new town. Thanksgiving will be upon us soon, but I'm sure that afterwards you'll want to go back to school, won't you?"

Brya scrunched up her face. She hadn't missed school, really, and never felt like she learned anything there. Life was much more interesting to her than school ever was. She had attended a girls' school in Trinity, where she was required to wear uniforms and be a proper young lady. A couple of times Brya had to be disciplined by the headmaster. Daddy had never approved of her 'classroom behavior.'

"Um, well, I *guess* I should go back to school, Grandma."

"Yes dear, you should. Our town is small. You'll see the schoolhouse right around the corner. You might want to walk by and take a look." Grandma Eugenia stopped what she was doing and looked straight at Brya. "I'm terribly sorry about what you've been through. We're heartbroken about your mama, and we miss her terribly." Eugenia couldn't control her tears. She touched the corners of her eyes with the dish towel, then excused herself. Brya, not knowing what to say, wandered around the house. Sadness overwhelmed her. There was only one picture of her mama in the house, and it was hanging in their bedroom. It must be too painful to look around and see pictures of their daughter. There wasn't one picture of her daddy. Brya wondered why, but decided to leave that topic alone. She went upstairs to get ready for her walk.

Bundled up in her gray wool coat, Brya kissed Eugenia good-bye, promising to be home by lunchtime.

It was a crisp, fall day. The air was cold and clear. She noticed that the oak trees had dressed themselves up in vibrant colors, and their leaves had fallen all around. When she picked up a red one to admire its beauty, a voice came from behind, "Hello."

Brya quickly turned, and there stood Holden with his hands in his coat pocket, smiling.

"Hello, Holden," she said shyly. "What are you doing here?"

"I stopped by your house and your grandmother said you'd just left for a walk. I figured Mr. Gilmore would be busy, and you might want someone to show you around."

She glanced up into those gorgeous brown eyes, and took a deep swallow, "That would be very nice."

Holden had taken a fancy to her. He couldn't stop staring. He was five years older and could get any girl in town. But he had never felt this way about any of them.

Eugenia, on the other hand, had told Brya that the young women in the town chased after him all the time, but he never acted interested.

As they strolled through the streets, Brya asked Holden lots of questions. She always did that, though. She had a way of getting anything she wanted. Her parents used to say that she'd make a good politician's wife.

Holden graduated high school but never went to college. Instead, he helped his daddy at their general store until the day would come when he had saved enough money to buy a farm and raise white-legged chickens. When the drought was over, he also planned to raise 'rattlesnake watermelons.' His grandpa had given him a barrel full of dry seeds before he died.

"I'm keeping them till I can start my first bumper crop," Holden said. "Then I'm going to make lots of money."

"What on God's earth is a rattlesnake watermelon?" Brya thought he was pulling her leg like Brock used to do.

"That is a watermelon that has light green stripes on it. Haven't you ever seen one?"

"Oh sure I have, lots of them," she replied sarcastically.

"Mark my words, one day this funny idea's going to make me rich."

"Sure it is, Holden, and I'm going to be the queen of England!"

"Maybe you will, Brya. Maybe you will."

"How can anyone in their right mind want to raise chickens, let alone live around them?" she asked. "And growing plants that look like snakes . . . you're a strange one!"

Holden chuckled.

Eventually they walked over to the schoolhouse that she would be attending. It was a far cry from her private school in Trinity. This wooden schoolhouse was on one level with several classrooms. Each room had desks in the middle, with a big blackboard behind the teacher's desk. Brya knew she was going to freeze in there because none of the wooden floorboards were nailed firmly together. Oh well, what else was she going to do? She was going to have to start school when her grandparents told her to.

Holden walked Brya back to the house. She felt awkward because she didn't know what she was going to do with him once they got there. She was relieved when he said that he had work to do for his father and needed to go. She liked him, but he was so handsome that he made her feel uneasy—and uneasy wasn't a feeling she was used to having. It was noon as she walked into the house, just in time for another meal. If she kept this up, she'd be as round as her sweet grandma.

"Brya, please pick up that wooden spoon on the counter and stir this soup. My hands are full."

"All right, Grandma."

"Did you take your tour of Cimarron?"

"Yes, I did, and guess who came with me?"

"It wouldn't be Holden Hunter, would it?"

Brya blushed, finding it hard to look Eugenia in the eye. "Yes, ma'am."

"Isn't he a nice young man?"

"Oh yes, he sure is."

"His family has lived down the street from us for over thirty years. Patch and I knew of Holden before he was born, and he's turned out to be not only handsome, but a decent and kind young man. He'll be a nice friend for you, dear."

They sat down to their lunch of white bean soup, biscuits, and honey. Brya stayed home the rest of the day, studying the new Sears catalog, and listening to soap operas on the radio. Her guess was that her grandma would knit and sew and stay glued to her radio every afternoon, Patch would be at the bank weekdays, and most of their meals would be eaten at home.

It was boring here with no brothers or sisters, but what was she to do? They would be separated until they grew up and could move closer to each other. Occasionally, the image of Holden ran through her mind as she lay sprawled on the parlor floor. He was older and would never be interested in her because she was too young. Brya dismissed her thoughts, and tried to get involved with the mystery on the radio.

When Grandpa Patch returned in the evening, he was adamant about Brya starting school as soon as possible.

"You've already missed enough," he said, peering over his glasses and shaking his finger at her.

She reluctantly agreed. "I'll start tomorrow if that's what you want." She started to go upstairs to bed when Patch interrupted her.

"Before you go to sleep, I need to tell you something."

"Yes, Grandpa?" She walked back over to him and sat down on the floor next to his feet. He pulled out his pipe and lit it.

"After your family's estate was settled, each child was left with some money—five hundred dollars, to be exact. It is extraordinary in this day and age to have that much cash, especially for a young girl. For your first lesson in business, I want to teach you to save money. Look at some of the things you've seen on the drive here. I don't ever want to see you living like that." He handed over some bills in a jar. "Put it away in your closet where you'll forget about it. Because of the raging Depression, I don't want you to put any currency in the bank just yet."

Brya studied the jar closely. It was all she had left other than her mama's daybed.

"Your money will be safe for now," Patch continued. "You'll want to think of keeping it for something important. Otherwise, I don't want you spending it. When you are thinking about using it, remember this old adage my father taught me: 'Never let your emotion overshadow your reason on anything you do.' Take good care of yourself and your money, Brya. If you do that, you'll always be safe."

She clutched the container against her bosom, answering in a mature voice, "Each night before I go to sleep, I'll repeat that saying over and over. I promise that I won't touch the money."

She took the small jelly jar, gave both grandparents a hug, and went off to her room. She hid it on the upper shelf of her closet, and repeated the statement over and over again. With the money safely tucked away, she crawled under the soft sheets and turned her thoughts toward more interesting things, like her new friend, Holden.

Brya awoke bright and early; Patch made sure of that. He wanted her to get to school on time. She had washed her hair the night before in case she ran into Holden. The tiredness was finally leaving her face. Patch agreed to take her to school before going to work and would introduce her to the teacher, Miss Grisholm. Oo, Miss Gruesome, she thought.

She hugged Eugenia good-bye; she would see her at home for lunch. The morning was cold and blustery, so Brya clutched her coat around her neck. She enjoyed watching the colored leaves swirl around her. Her heart began to race as she got close to the school. She had to meet new people and make new friends. After all that she had been through, she didn't really want to meet anyone.

As Patch and Brya walked into the schoolhouse, a tight-lipped, tall, thin woman approached the two of them. Her black hair was tied up in a bun. This lady has got to be Miss Gruesome.

"Good morning, Miss Grisholm," Patch stated with his usual style and elegance. "I would like you to meet my granddaughter, Brya. She'll be joining you this year."

"Good morning Mr. Gilmore," she said as her breath nearly knocked Brya over. "Good morning," Miss Grisholm said to Brya, giving her a stare as she looked down her nose at her. "You know, Brya, your mother used to go to school here. She was a good student, so I expect you will be the same. And how is your mother, child?"

Brya froze . . . No one had asked her about Mama Beatrice and she began to stammer, "My mama . . . my mama . . . well, she just died, Miss Grisholm." She looked down at the floor.

"I'm sorry, child," Miss Grisholm said. The teacher laid her long fingers on her shoulder. Brya looked up into her face. Behind all the wrinkles and aged eyes, Brya could see some compassion, but her new teacher still looked like a witch. Why would anyone want to learn from her?

Patch gave Brya a hug and left for the bank. "Brya, please sit down next to Will Smith over there." Miss Grisholm pointed toward a little boy in the back. Next to him was an empty desk. She gave a quick smile to Will as she started to sit down, but he didn't pay her any mind. "Here are all the books that you'll need," Miss Grisholm said sharply.

Brya politely said 'thank you' as a pile of old books was dropped on her desk. She began to cough from the dust.

This was the beginning of her career at Miss Grisholm's schoolhouse. It was plain and ordinary, and different from anything Brya knew. Here, the upper grades were all in one classroom, and the boys and girls looked poor. In Trinity, Brya's schoolhouse was brick and had lots of classrooms for the different ages of children. Though they wore uniforms, there wasn't a poor student in the bunch.

As the days passed, Holden often showed up to walk Brya home after school. She wondered if he had made it a point to coincide his work schedule with hers. He didn't always come, but her anticipation to see him grew with each day. After school was out, she would wait about ten minutes. When he was there, she was happy; when he was not, she pouted.

Brya's philosophy used to be that one couldn't learn anything unless it was in a fine setting. But being in Cimarron at Miss Grisholm's school had taught her differently. She *could* learn no matter where she was.

One chilly November day, Miss Grisholm punished her by sending her outside to sit on a bunch of logs behind the schoolhouse. Brya had been badgering Will Smith, so she had to stay there and think about what she had done wrong.

Brya was wearing a plaid wool skirt, red sweater, and white knee socks. As she was sitting on the logs, she suddenly felt a pinch on the back of her leg. She jumped up and saw a small, clear scorpion scoot off into the wood pile. She began to feel woozy so she headed back into the classroom to tell Miss Grisholm what had happened. Everyone was alarmed but Miss Grisholm, who sprang into action. She sent Will to fetch the local doctor, laid Brya down on the cold wooden floor, and pulled out some Red Man chewing tobacco from her desk drawer.

Miss Grisholm shoved a plug of tobacco into her mouth and chewed profusely, until it was all wet and sloppy. Before Brya knew it, she spit it into her hand and slapped the nasty stuff on the back of her leg. She said that the tobacco would draw out the scorpion's poison—and it did. By the time Will and the doctor came running back to the schoolhouse, Brya was already doing better from Miss Grisholm's home remedy. That witch lady saved her life, and her well-kept secret would now be the talk of the town.

Before Brya knew it, Thanksgiving arrived. The town of Cimarron saw its first light flurry of snow and Eugenia and Patch invited the Hunters over for Thanksgiving dinner. For twenty years, the two families had shared this holiday. Now Brya was the new addition to the gathering. Eugenia had transformed the house into a festival of smells, from her cranberry sauce to her pumpkin pie and rosemary bread. Early in the day, Holden brought over a twenty-pound fresh turkey to be cooked in Eugenia's oven. Maud, his mama, would come down later to baste it with sweet butter until it turned golden brown. The table was set with the grandparents' finest decorations. The tablecloth was made by

Eugenia's Mama Agnes. It was a cranberry red lace with matching napkins, so it could be used for both Thanksgiving and Christmas. All the silver and china was a gift to Patch and Eugenia from Beatrice.

After the final touches were put on the table and the candles were lit, it was time to eat. Everyone was in the dining room but Brya, who was still in her room getting ready. Patch called to her, and shortly she came down, apologizing for keeping everyone waiting.

She had kept one formal dress made of oyster white taffeta. It had a light blue satin sash tied in a perfect bow in the back, and around her neck lay a single strand of her mama's pearls. Brya pinched her cheeks so that they were slightly flushed, and her hair cascaded in loose curls down her back. Nothing was out of place.

Holden almost fell off his chair when he saw her but tried to hide his feelings so no one would notice. She smiled at everyone, spreading a lavender scent through the air as she breezed into the room. She had been brought up with class and dignity, and people noticed.

However, it was a sad Thanksgiving for Brya, even though she tried to make the best of it. She missed her brothers and sisters. As the snow fell outside, and the fireplace warmed the parlor, everyone enjoyed the delicious meal. The light hit the stained glass window in the dining room in a way that gave it the feeling of a cozy church.

After Brya scraped her plate, her eyes stayed fixed on it. Suddenly she became upset and started to cry. She realized it was the same rosebud china that she had cookies on the day her daddy killed himself. She pushed the plate away violently, and for one moment, saw bright, red blood instead of roses. Holden put his arm around her, trying to comfort her. She buried her head in his chest and sobbed. No one spoke.

Marriage

By spring, 1932, Brya had fallen hard for Holden. They were inseparable. She knew that she was too young to be seriously in love, but she couldn't help the feelings she carried in her heart. Perhaps she needed someone to cling to, but then again, maybe Holden would be the love of her life. Could it be that she was bored living in Cimarron and wanted out? Whatever it was, the feeling was real to her, and she knew Holden loved her more than anything.

Brya couldn't sleep well anymore, and neither could he. They talked about a future together and both felt ready. As soon as Holden could muster up the courage to talk with her grandpa about getting married, he would.

She bet he wouldn't take long.

❦

One evening, as Eugenia was finishing up in the kitchen, and Patch and Brya were listening to the evening news on the radio, the doorbell rang. Brya got up from the sofa and answered it. There stood Holden.

"What are you doing here?" she said.

"Brya, I need to talk with your grandpa, please," he said abruptly, walking past her into the hallway.

"Just a minute, then," she said. "Grandpa, Holden's here to speak with you." She turned to wink at him and knew exactly why he was there.

Patch came into the hall removing his spectacles. "Yes, young man, what can I do for you?"

"Well, um, can I speak with you in private, sir?" Holden's hands were shaking.

"Certainly, son."

The two men walked into the parlor, and Brya trailed close behind.

"Brya," Holden said, "I'd like for you to go into the other room, please."

"But . . ."

"Just do as I ask, sweetheart."

"All right then," she said, shutting the parlor door. She quickly put her ear against it to listen.

First they made small talk. Then Holden blurted out that he wanted to ask for Brya's hand in marriage.

Oh my gosh, he said it! she realized, as she slid down the door in surprise.

Patch must have been in shock, too, because he was quiet—and he was never quiet.

Holden said that he had been in love from the very first moment he laid eyes on her.

Now she was really swooning.

She guessed Patch had recovered his wits because he reminded Holden of their ages and how young Brya was. He also wanted to know what kind of future Holden could possibly offer Brya?

Her nervous beau launched into his sermon about the chicken farm he was going to buy with all the money he had saved. Brya sure hoped she could handle raising chickens. Her hands had never touched a live one before. But she was so in love with this man, she knew that they could make anything work.

Next, Patch got real practical and wanted to know how much money Holden had, especially in this depression, and he reminded him that his granddaughter was used to only the finest things in life. He didn't believe that this young fellow could support her properly.

Without hesitation, Holden told him that by the time they got married (and she did love how he phrased that in the positive), he would have over one thousand dollars saved.

Patch started clearing his throat, trying to digest the news, but then seemed to take Holden seriously.

"What do you plan to raise on this farm of yours, son?"

Brya smiled and tried not to jump up and down, because right now, Holden was ahead in the discussion. She took a deep breath and calmed herself.

"I want us to move to Muddy Boggy Creek, Oklahoma, where I plan on raising white leghorn chickens. I hear that it's an affordable place to start a farm. After I get the chicken farm to a profitable stage, sir, I want to grow rattlesnake watermelons. I can't do anything about that until the drought's over, but I have all the seeds I need from my grandfather. I'm just waiting till the time is right."

"Muddy Boggy Creek is an affordable place to be but that's because it has been hit so hard by the Depression, son." Patch said. "Life is rough there. The dust storms have driven out families and destroyed their farms. You have an uphill battle ahead of you and it worries me. I can't imagine Brya happy in such a place. And do you really feel that you'll have enough money, and the ability to make a go of your dream?"

Holden took a deep breath, and chose his words carefully, "Sir, you of all people know that the time to purchase a property is when the price is down. I can get more for my money. I plan on making the farming business profitable so we can sell and I can give Brya the nice home she deserves. I would never take her to a place like Muddy Boggy Creek if I didn't think that I could make a go of it. Besides, we can't stay here because Cimarron is not a farming community. Brya and I can make a wonderful life together wherever we go. She's had so much pain; I would never do anything to hurt her in any way."

Brya, about to break down and cry, heard Grandpa stand up and announce, "I'm saddened that you plan on moving away, but I understand the drive young people have today to make it on their own. I remember when I did it myself."

"Young lady," Patch called, "I know that you're listening behind that door. Will you please come in here? And go get your grandma, too."

Brya jumped up slamming against the parlor door and yelled, "Grandma, hurry! Grandpa wants to talk to us."

Eugenia came scuttling down the hallway, and Brya pushed open the door with her sweaty palms. "Yes, Grandpa?" She batted her eyes at both men. Her grandma walked in with a curious look on her face.

"Brya," Patch said, looking her straight in the eyes, "I won't repeat the conversation because I know you've heard all of it. What I will say is that I wish you all the best. I think you are both too young to get married, especially you, my dear granddaughter. However, Holden has planned for this for so long, my saying no won't help anything. And with the little I know about you, Brya, you won't let me say no, either. I am well aware that the stubborn Fitzgibbons and Gilmore blood flows through your veins. Your grandma and I give you our blessing, but *only* after you graduate."

Holden shook hands with Patch, and Brya gave her grandpa a giant kiss on the cheek. Eugenia was stunned. The young couple then kissed each other in front of the grandparents while they held hands. Afterwards, Brya could see a tear in the corner of her grandpa's eyes.

The next day was Saturday, and the Gilmore house was all atwitter with wedding talk. Brya wanted all of her brothers and sisters to be a part of the ceremony. It would be sometime in the late summer. She wanted Emilia to play the piano, Megan to be a bridesmaid, and for Brock and Duke to help out in general. Patch allowed her to call all of them.

Emilia was surprised and happy for her, but sad that she wouldn't be able to come. She was finally able to study with Ignace Paderewski, the famous concert pianist, and would not give up this long-awaited opportunity. Emilia explained that he was getting old, and would no longer return to the United States to teach and give concerts. The time to study with him was now. Brya understood her sister's dream but would miss her at her wedding. They wished each other well, and once again, said good-bye.

After lots of attempts, Brya finally reached her brother Brock on the telephone.

"Brock, I'm getting married! Can you come?"

"Sis, I'd love to, but I'm graduating from military school in a few months, and then I'm on my way to Venezuela to work in the oil fields."

"Why don't you go to work in the Oklahoma City oil field?"

"You mean the one that opened up in 1928?"

"How the heck do I know when it opened? You're the oil expert."

"Brya, remember the last night we were all together—when I told you that I was going to South America and would come back a millionaire? I haven't changed my mind. I'll make the Fitzgibbons name strong again, you'll see. One day we'll be together again, I promise. Stay well."

Brya knew better than to try to stop her younger brother, who was much like herself. She understood that after the death of their daddy, he needed to put distance between himself and Trinity.

Something was strange about Duke when Brya talked to him. He was different. She could tell by the way he spoke that he was more indolent than ever. It didn't look as though he would be attending the wedding, either.

After her parents were gone, Brya told herself that she wouldn't count on anyone. Now she saw that, once again, she was right. So far, not one of her brothers or sisters could make it to the wedding. She knew that she couldn't look back, and had to go on, but she didn't think that she'd have to let go of her brothers and sisters, too.

There was just one more sister to call and that was Megan, in Oklahoma City. Brya hoped that at least she could attend. Megan was surprised, but after getting permission from her Aunt Claire, promised to be there as Brya's maid of honor.

The wedding date was set for the first of August, 1932, on Brya's nineteenth birthday. She wanted it that way. She chose to be married in the chapel where her parents were wed. Patch telephoned Rev. Riley to see if that day was available. It was. Brya wanted a sunset wedding—in the coolest part of the day—followed by a party under the stars. It would be the most romantic evening anyone had seen in Cimarron since her parents' wedding.

After Patch hung up the telephone, he commented, "I'm fortunate to be in a fairly good financial situation, Brya. You acquired expensive taste growing up in Trinity. Thank goodness I can manage to pay for your wedding. I only hope Holden will be able to afford you."

"I hope so, too, Grandpa."

Brya and her grandma couldn't wait to start working on the wedding gown. Eugenia knew a wonderful seamstress right there in Cimarron who could design it. She didn't live far away from them either. But first, they needed to search out some fabrics to get an idea of what Brya wanted. So, early on Monday morning, Patch dropped them off at the train station and they headed to Oklahoma City.

Brya had telephoned ahead to Megan and Aunt Claire and asked if they knew a good fabric shop. Her aunt suggested they all meet downtown on Broadway at one of the best mercantile stores for fine fabrics. Nearby was a hotel where they could stay. Eugenia and Brya had six months to have every part of the wedding designed and completed. They had their work cut out for them.

Megan now knew why her sister had not had time to come visit. The man in her life was her priority.

The days they chose to go shopping were humid ones in early spring. The thick, moist air made it difficult to breathe.

Mr. Scarber, the owner of the fabric store, was a little man with gray hair and a pencil-thin mustache. You could tell he smoked because his fingers were stained yellow, but he was cordial and helpful, and knew when to leave the ladies alone.

Looking at fabrics took up the better part of the second day. They wanted the right sense of balance between the decor and the gown. Brya decided that her colors were to be pink, off-white and white—good summer colors. They found gorgeous off-white satin for the body of the gown. Netting and handmade brocade work would be used for finishing touches. She wanted the dress to be form-fitting which, for a young girl, was scandalous. But Brya didn't care. She saw the style in a magazine and it was glamorous. To compliment it, she would need a long train and veil.

"My poor Megan, you'll be doing all the work carrying it down the aisle. Try not to trip," Brya teased.

"You're funny, Brya. Real funny. You just find me a nice young man if you really want to pay me back."

"There's always Mr. Scarber at the mercantile store."

"Not exactly the kind of man I'm looking for."

On the third day, Eugenia and Brya said good-bye to Megan and Claire and rode the train back to Cimarron. Their next stop would be the florist. Brya wanted to discuss the bouquets for her and her sister. She was partial to lilies of the valley, simple flowers, delicate and dainty. Eugenia and Brya agreed that with the satin gown, this flower would be perfect—and it was in season in the summer. Eugenia marveled at her granddaughter's good taste. She said that Beatrice had a natural talent that way, and it had definitely rubbed off on her daughter.

For their last errand, they stopped in at Mrs. Wicker's house, the dress designer. Most designers were persnickety, so Brya hoped that she could tolerate the lady. She calmed down when Eugenia told her that Mrs. Wicker designed her mama's bridal gown. She must have been young then, because she was old now. They discussed the style of the dress, and Mrs. Wicker made a face as she looked through the glasses that were perched on her nose.

"Aren't you a little young, *dear,* to be wearing such a revealing dress?" said Mrs. Wicker.

Brya flashed her eyes at her, and said, "I don't think so, *ma'am.*"

Mrs. Wicker wouldn't be making another snide comment to her. The elderly seamstress took all necessary measurements and in the course of it, became very friendly.

"My dear, you have such a petite body and erect posture. You'll make a beautiful bride."

"Thank you," she said curtly.

By this time, Eugenia and Brya were ready to go home. Patch picked them up at Mrs. Wicker's late that evening. Their feet were tired and swollen.

"I don't understand why women spend days at the stores, then return home feeling beat up and tired," Patch said.

Brya leaned forward and rubbed her grandpa's shoulders, "It will all be worth it. You'll understand when you see the finished product."

Patch chuckled. "Well Brya, you deserve it. It's the least I can do for the daughter of my only child."

The wedding plans continued to occupy everyone, even through Brya's graduation. There were trips to the engravers, interviews with musicians, and discussions with the minister. The list was endless. She and Holden were hardly together these days. He was working longer hours to make even more money, which left Eugenia and Brya to battle with the details of the wedding and reception. But it was hard on them to not be together as they had been, before the proposal.

They finally planned an evening to create their guest list. When Holden and his parents arrived after dinner, Brya hugged him long and hard. It felt like he had been out of town on an extended trip. One of the things she loved about him was how calm and warm he made her feel. How could she be without him, or have another man in her life? Well, these weren't possibilities, so she kicked the ideas out of her mind. She and her fiancé were bound to be together forever, have lots of babies, and become rich on chickens and rattlesnake watermelons.

After spending two grueling hours on the guest list, Holden and Brya put down their pencils and excused themselves to go out for a stroll.

The wedding day was only two months away. As they walked hand in hand down the street, sparks flew through both of them. Holden was having a difficult time controlling his desires towards Brya, and she felt the same. They wanted each other terribly. After they reached a dark, remote spot at the end of the street, where no one could see them, Holden laid her down in the soft grass and began to kiss her neck. His hands slid underneath her sweater to caress her firm bosom. He knew that she was a virgin, and said that this made her even more desirable. His hands entered her wet panties as Brya felt his hardness press against her.

"Holden, stop, please. We have to wait for our wedding night." It took all her strength to pull his hand away.

"But I want you so badly, Brya. I want all of you now. I can't take this much longer."

"Honey, this isn't the right time or place."

He rolled off of her, disappointed, "I understand, sweetheart, I just love you so much."

The next months were difficult for them. Holden worked harder and harder, but now purposefully stayed away. He couldn't take being close without wanting more of her.

Brya felt the same about him, but she wouldn't do anything to jeopardize the family name. She had experienced a lot of scandal and embarrassment in her life, and wanted no more of it.

❧

When Brya's big day finally arrived, she woke up crying. She wept for her family, and ached to be near them. Her parents would have given her the grandest of all weddings, she was sure of that. She wanted her mama to be there, smoothing her hair and helping her dress. Instead, she was relying on herself, and that was frightening. As the tears rolled down her cheeks, she nestled into her satin pillow, and daydreamed about her carefree childhood. She was running along the edge of the Trinity River with her brothers and sisters to see who could find the most four-leaf clovers. She watched her parents relax beneath the branches of an old weeping willow tree, observing their children at play. A picnic basket sat on the blanket, full of Eusabia's scrumptious sandwiches and cakes. She ached to feel all

50

that love and closeness again, and to be that happy, carefree little girl.

Her only hope was that, with Holden, she could have it back. She wanted her white knight to save her from the pain. Holden was her hero, just like her daddy had been. After all, he was older and wiser. Their children would be beautiful, and they'd create a perfect life together as a family. She sighed, then got up to face her day with this romantic picture in her mind. She wiped her tears, and turned her thoughts toward all that needed to be accomplished before she made her grand entrance. Besides, she couldn't go down the aisle with her eyes swollen and red.

The day before Brya's wedding, Megan arrived in Cimarron, with Aunt Claire and Uncle Earl. They were staying at the Pioneer Hotel downtown. Patch would bring Megan and Claire to the house so the girls could spend the day together and Claire could give Eugenia a hand.

Brya washed her face, brushed her teeth, and skipped down the stairs to a steaming plateful of buttermilk pancakes. Eugenia was grinning from ear to ear as she fetched cinnamon rolls from the oven.

"You'll need all your strength today, my dear," she said as she set before Brya a breakfast fit for a ranch hand.

"You're so thoughtful. You and Grandpa have been the best grandparents a girl could have. Thank you for taking me into your life." Brya had butterflies in her stomach but managed to swallow enough food to make them go away.

"You've brought us a great deal of happiness, child, and we hope that you and Holden won't forget us. We promise to come to Muddy Boggy Creek and visit y'all." Eugenia gave her a squeeze.

The two of them discussed Brya's appointments that day. The hairdresser was coming to the house, along with the manicurist. The two sisters would get dressed together.

How Brya was getting to the church was a surprise from Patch, who promised that it would be unforgettable.

After the breakfast dishes were washed and the last one put away, Eugenia left to check on the flower arrangements to make sure that the florist had chosen the right ones for the wedding and reception. The chapel was next door to the town hall, where the reception would be, so it would be easy for her to do both.

"What's Grandpa doing today?" Brya asked.

Eugenia laughed. "I imagine he'll be doing what all men do on a wedding day, and that's having a drink and talking about why you two shouldn't get married. I'm sure your Uncle Earl will join him in that. It's a tradition, you know. I just hope he comes home in time to put on his tuxedo."

They both went about their business because they knew they could trust Patch to show up on time.

❧

Megan was a sight for sore eyes by the time she arrived at the house. It had been three long months since Brya had seen her sister, and last night's short visit was hardly enough to catch up.

"Oh, Megan!" Brya said, throwing her arms around her. "You look so beautiful." She played with her sister's shiny, brown hair and flipped her pearl necklace. "I can't wait to tell you everything. Let's go up to my room because we have oodles to talk about before the ceremony."

Brya grabbed her sister's hand and began to dash up the stairs to her private sanctuary.

"You girls!" Eugenia yelled, as they flew out of sight. "The manicurist will be here in an hour, so you decide who goes first. On second thought, Brya, you go first because the hairdresser needs to tend to all of that long hair of yours."

"Yes ma'am," they responded in unison. "I promise we'll be ready when she gets here," Brya shouted back. They giggled and slammed the door.

"I can't wait to meet Holden, Brya," Megan said as they flopped onto the messy bed. She held both of Brya's hands, which were cold and tense. "From your letters, he sounds so dreamy. One day, I hope I can find a nice husband and be as happy as you are."

"You will, you will. If anyone deserves it, you do. You've always been the sweetest and most loyal one in the family. I'm sure that the right man will come along for you. Oh Megan, I'm so in love with Holden. He's everything I ever wanted and everything I need. I'm going to be rich again, sis—and Holden will spoil us all, just like Daddy did."

Megan let go of her hands a moment, trying to digest what she had just heard. She reached over to open the locket hanging around Brya's neck, the one that she'd given her the day she left Trinity. Originally, it contained a picture of the two of them, but it had been replaced with photos of their parents. Megan swallowed and closed the locket. "What happened to our pictures, Brya?"

"I can always see you. But I'll never see our parents again."

Megan patted her shoulder and said nothing more.

Aunt Claire went to the hotel for a nap before getting dressed. Megan and Brya spent the afternoon beautifying themselves and talking about their lives since they'd been apart. Megan was tired of Oklahoma and wanted to go to California; she had heard it was the "land of opportunity." There she hoped to find her mate, and settle down. Brya thought that was a fine idea. It was far away but the ocean sounded like a wonderful place to visit. She imagined her children playing at the seashore and loving it.

The afternoon flew by and before they knew it, it was coming up to the time to go to the church. With their hair, fingernails, and pedicures completed, the moment had come to put on their dresses. Megan's dress was made of pink satin and the bodice was intertwined with matching lace. Her skirt was long and tulip-shaped to hide her hips. After she sent her measurements, Brya helped design the dress so it would enhance her best attributes.

The form-fitting bridal gown was breathtaking. Brya's hair fell in soft curls all around, and her lips and cheeks looked like they'd been kissed by pink roses. She felt like a fairy princess.

When they heard a loud honk outside, the two sisters raced to the window. There stood Patch in his tuxedo, grinning from ear to ear and proud as a peacock. He had borrowed his partner's sleek Model A Ford, the kind with a picnic basket on the back of it. The basket was filled with summer flowers. The girls waved at their grandpa and motioned to him that they were coming down. As they left the bedroom, Eugenia greeted them looking as lovely as Brya had ever seen her, and so happy. She was wearing a lavender satin dress with shimmering beads dotted about the bodice. The formal dresses swished as they walked down the staircase. At the last moment, Grandma gave Brya her blue garter for 'something borrowed, something blue.' It had been hers the day she and Patch married, forty-five years ago. Brya slid the garter onto the upper part of her leg.

Patch helped them into the car, and traffic stopped to stare as they drove down the road.

As usual, Brya was running a little late. When they arrived at the church, they could hear the organ music resounding out into the street. Patch led all of them to the side entrance and said he'd be back shortly to walk Brya down the aisle. There hadn't been any rehearsal because

Megan couldn't make it to Cimarron on time. The ceremony would be another complete surprise.

Waiting there in the back of the church was Bartholomew Jones, the town florist, whose cologne competed with the sweet-smelling flowers. He held Brya's bridal bouquet of lillies, and Megan's white pom pom mums. Everything was tied together with pink satin ribbon, which trailed down their dresses. There were little handles inside the bouquets so they wouldn't drop them as they headed down the aisle. He handed each of them their flowers and wished his best to Brya.

The bride was getting nervous, and slightly flushed. Eugenia stroked her cheek trying to comfort and reassure her. Then, the whole shebang moved quickly. Grandpa came through the door with Holden's best man to escort Eugenia down the aisle. He let them know that the church was full and everyone was ready to begin. The group walked into the church foyer. Eugenia took a deep breath and locked her arm inside that of the young man. They proceeded down the aisle. Megan was next. She was so busy flirting with Holden's brother Mark, who decided to stay in the back with the women, that she almost forgot to go down the aisle. He was not quite as handsome as Holden, but his smile was devastating. When Megan reached the front of the church, Brya knew the time had come, finally, for her to embark on a new journey. "The Wedding March" played, and the audience rose from their seats.

Holden looked like a Greek god as he stood at the front of the church, watching Brya. He had waited so long for this moment. Brya could tell that he was relieved she was there. She hung on to her grandpa as they began to walk. She and Patch smiled at each other and the crowd sighed. When they came to the end of their walk, Rev. Riley voiced some brief words to the congregation. To the bride and groom he said, "Who gives this woman in matrimony?"

Patch replied, with a crack in his voice, "Her grand-mother and I do." He then kissed Brya's hand, and delicately passed her over to Holden. Holden smiled down at her as she reached inside his arm and gently brushed against him. Just then, Judge Teesdale's cane hit the hard surface of the floor. He must have had a few too many drinks before the ceremony and had fallen asleep. Brya heard a few chuckles, and the rest of the ceremony was a blur.

Once the simple gold bands were placed on their fingers, and they said "I do," Rev. Riley declared, "I now pronounce you man and wife." Holden gently lifted Brya's veil and looked deep into his wife's eyes. He kissed her tenderly. Megan began crying, which set off the other women seated nearby. Rev. Riley continued, "May I present to the town of Cimarron, Oklahoma, Mr. and Mrs. Holden Hunter."

The thundering organ music started up again. In a whirlwind, they were down the aisle and out the door, headed for the town hall.

While they were being photographed on the steps of the hall, people gathered around to watch. The photographer was excited about his newest gadget—the flashbulb. It meant that people could be photographed indoors and at night without setting up special lights. Holden and Brya smiled for the camera, hoping that it would be over soon. She wanted to get on with the reception, and Holden wanted to get on with leaving.

Patch and Eugenia knew nothing about music but the Hunters had heard about a new string band. As Megan, Mark, Holden, and Brya entered the building, laughing and holding hands, they heard a guitar tuning up. They saw the three-piece band that they had procured. The group had come from Oklahoma City. A tall, lanky fiddle player was bent forward, tuning up his instrument, while the stubby-fingered banjo player picked at his. Some kind of new equipment was behind the guitar player that made the sound come out even louder. The guitar was plugged into it. All sorts of new-fangled things were being made these days. Who could keep up?

Pink satin streamers and hundreds of bows filled the room and gave it an air of gaiety. The tablecloths were made of crisp, white embossed damask with napkins to match, tied with pink ribbon. They had selected a fine menu from the caterer, and since they were a young couple, there was no liquor served, just fresh fruit punch and tea. Patch didn't want to run the risk of being raided by authorities anyway. He said with Prohibition still hanging in the balance, a wedding was no place to risk a problem.

The music started, and as the newlyweds greeted everyone, the party began. It was a warm August night, and soon all the stars came out. It seemed as though the earth and sky orchestrated their own night music to make this a memorable wedding. The doors to the hall were flung open on all sides, and the ceiling fans were whirring, so everyone would be comfortable while dancing to the string band. Children danced with children, old people with young, and elderly married couples danced close, remembering when. Megan and Holden's brother, Mark, were having a good time with one another, while Holden and Brya held each other tight. They danced and danced until Brya had to remove her white satin shoes to rub her sore feet. Her new husband, concerned, helped her sit down to rest.

Everyone was enjoying themselves, down to the last piece of pink-flowered wedding cake with ice cream. Brya didn't eat much dinner, and couldn't muster up an appetite to eat any cake, either. As the evening wore on, her thoughts turned more toward their first night together. She had never been with Holden "like that" before. Eugenia discussed a few things with her shortly before the wedding. She told her to always wear clean underwear and never let her husband see soiled undergarments. Take lots of baths and always smell good. Sleep with your husband, if not every night, every other night, because you don't want him to have a wandering eye. But what would he expect of her tonight? This all seemed so complicated and mechanical. Actually, it seemed like a gosh awful amount of work. As Brya rested in her chair, she occasionally glanced at Holden as he listened to the music. She was nervous.

As the party wound down, the newlyweds left the reception, ducking to avoid the last handful of rice. Holden's brother Mark drove up to the entrance of the hall, honking profusely. He had borrowed a navy blue and cream-colored Model A Ford with spoked rims. The leather had been shined up, and there was a large sign in the back window that read, *JUST MARRIED*. Dragging from the bumper were several pairs of old shoes. Mark was always full of spirit and surprise, and tonight was no exception. He motioned for Holden and Brya to climb in so that he could take them to the hotel. They escaped for their honeymoon weekend at the Hotel Bernard, the most elegant place in town.

Built in 1888, the Bernard was the first hotel in Cimarron. It took care of cowboys, prominent railroad men, and regular travelers. Three railroads crossed by there: the Katy, the Missouri-Pacific, and the Iron Mountain, which in time, had brought all types of folks to the area. Holden told Brya that the bridal suite would be something to see.

She was getting fidgety as her husband checked in. While they were walking upstairs, he tried to make small talk to make her feel more comfortable. When they got to the bridal chamber, he swept her up in his muscled arms and carried her over the threshold. This took Brya by surprise, but she giggled and looked dreamily into his eyes. He cradled her in his arms while they walked around and admired the beautiful room.

It was a grand bridal suite with a fainting couch and a claw-footed bathtub, trimmed in gold. The canopy over the four-poster bed was made of old-fashioned white lace. The bed was filled with soft, fluffy down.

Brya's nervousness began to subside, and she felt warm and safe, just like when her daddy used to hold her when she was crying. Holden sat her down, took her face in his hands, and kissed her tenderly.

Behind them on the vanity sat an ice bucket with a chilled bottle of champagne. A note from Mark said: "I stole it, enjoy it, it's your night to howl!" They roared with laughter because only Mark would do something like that. He even remembered two glasses. Brya had never had a drink in her life, but Holden had.

In a debonair way, he bowed and asked, "May I pour you a glass, my beautiful bride?"

"You may, my handsome husband," she said as she curtsied, pretending to be a fair young maiden.

Holden popped the cork. Since he wasn't that good at opening the bottle, the champagne fizzed everywhere. Brya caught some of it in her glass and he poured her the rest. He toasted, took a sip of his drink, and kissed her with wet, tasty champagne lips.

"Oh, that tastes good, kiss me again," she said, forcing her pursed lips out to meet her husband's.

The two of them sipped champagne and talked about the wedding for a little while, as Holden watched her closely. "Would you like for me to run a bubble bath for you? It'll help you relax."

The champagne had affected her. "Yes," as she looked up at him with sleepy eyes.

Brya stood up quickly, tripped, giggled, then went to unpack some lavender bath oil to give him. Holden disappeared into the bathroom to draw a hot bath. While the tub was filling, he gave her a wedding present. She unwrapped a tiny package which held a bracelet in it. Dangling from a fourteen-carat gold chain was a rattlesnake watermelon seed encased in clear glass with gold around it. The card read, "Always treasure this, for in this seed lies our future. I'll always love you, Holden." Brya threw her arms around him and cried. This was the most special moment of her life.

Oddly enough, she had something similar made for him. She had taken the 'Fitzgibbons' soil' that Brock had given to her in an envelope when she left Trinity. A glassblower encased the loose dirt in a clear, glass paperweight for Holden's desk. The card read, "To my love. From my family's earth springs success. It is now yours. All my love, Brya." The two of them held each other close for a minute until Holden realized that the bathtub was about to over-flow. He ran to turn off the water.

She asked him to wait in the bedroom while she took off her clothes. Brya didn't want him to see her naked body before she immersed herself into the bubbles. She guessed she felt like a lot of women when they were with a man for the first time: extremely private and fearful. He reluctantly agreed, but he asked if she would allow him to give her a back rub after she was inside the bubbles. She sensed that would feel good and agreed. Holden handed Brya a full glass of champagne and she disappeared into the bathroom.

She carefully slipped off her bridal gown, veil, and undergarments, then stared into the mirror at her naked body. The bathroom smelled of lavender. As she wiped the steam off the mirror, she heard some soft music floating from the bedroom. Her husband had brought the radio along with him. She tied her long hair up with wedding combs and satin ribbons, but tips of blonde hair still touched her shoulders. As Brya turned sideways to study herself, her hand brushed over her pink nipples and then gently glided over her coarse pubic hair. How would a man touch her? Would it be like this? And would he be gentle? She shivered a little as she took a long sip of the champagne, set the glass on the floor where she could reach it, then stepped up into the bathtub, and sank into the bubbles. Slowly dripping the water over her with a wash cloth, she blew a few bubbles off her hand. She listened to the lilting jazz music and closed her eyes for a moment. "Brya, can I come in now?"

She quickly sat up with her forearms covering her chest and gulped, sliding back down to cover her body in bubbles. "Ye . . . yes, come in, Holden."

He opened the door, and smiled down at her. There he stood with his black wedding trousers on and an open shirt. His chest was tanned and muscled.

"Don't be afraid of me, Brya, I'm not going to hurt you." Holden knelt down at the edge of the bathtub and asked for the washcloth. She was shaking so much that her hands fumbled to find it. She handed it to her husband, who asked, "Brya, would you like your feet rubbed?"

She thought that this was an odd request, but said yes. He reached in and began rubbing her feet, right in the middle on the arch. That felt so good that she tingled all over. She teased him a little and put some bubbles on his head and tugged at his ear. He enjoyed the playfulness and allowed her to do whatever she felt comfortable doing. After he finished rubbing her feet, he moved to her shoulders. She was getting so relaxed, she felt like she was going to slide into the bubbles and drown. Holden massaged her shoulders and inched to the top of her breasts. Brya did not flinch. His hands slid over her pointed nipples and caressed them ever so gently. She rose to meet his mouth while she ran her wet hands over his chest. He felt so warm. Their breathing escalated as they fondled each other. After licking the water beads off her neck and the upper part of her back, his hand began a slow journey past her navel to her private parts. He successfully slipped a finger inside of her. When she flinched a little, he pulled his hand away, but she brought it back. Before all of the water was on the floor, Holden stopped and asked if he could see all of her standing before him. She hesitantly agreed and stood up.

"Brya, you are the most magnificent creature I have ever seen. Your waist is so small and your breasts are beautiful."

He held out a bath towel and wrapped her in it. This time, he swept her up and carried her to the bed. As he gently rolled her over, his tongue slithered down her spine and rotated in circles at the top of her buttocks. She moaned in ecstasy. When she turned over, all she could see was the large bulge in his wet trousers. He began to massage her again while she looked at the bulge. What did that *thing* look like?

Holden laid down on top of her and took her mouth in his. She began to writhe. The more he rubbed, the more she responded. Before she knew it, he took off his clothing and straddled her so that she could see his penis. It was so funny looking. How could that ever give a woman pleasure? He had her touch him there and it felt like rubber—warm and pliable.

Holden laid down on her again, this time opening her legs. He entered her gently and pushed against the hidden barrier that needed to be penetrated.

"I don't want to hurt you, Brya. Bite my shoulder if you need to."

She nodded.

He suddenly plunged himself into her and her long fingernails dug into his back. The pain was excruciating. She cried out and bit his shoulder.

"It won't feel like this again." he said. "I promise."

He stroked her head while she cried. She had been ready to lose her virginity but didn't realize she would feel so violated. Holden rolled off her. She was bleeding and scared.

"Oh Brya, my darlin' Brya, I don't want you to hurt."

Holden brought her a warm wash cloth to clean herself with. She wrapped herself in the towel and went into the bathroom to clean her private parts. When she finished, she went over and laid down next to him. She told him that she wanted to be with him again soon, but needed it to feel good like everything else had. She just wanted to get over how sore her insides felt. She nestled in his strong arms while he stroked her all over. She fell asleep, tired and content, ready to cope with becoming a married woman.

Holden woke her up the next morning, with his hard hugeness against her back. She rolled over and began to kiss him. They both became aroused and this time, when he entered her, it didn't hurt—even though she was still a little sore. He began to go up and down in her gently. She felt herself more and more wet down there. The feeling inside her was intense. She wrapped her legs around his back and he held her up to him. Shortly, she felt his warm rush, then an explosive sensation came over her that left her body trembling. This was the best feeling she'd ever had. Holden was grinning from ear to ear as he slowly pulled himself out. They held each other and kissed and kissed. The waiting was finally over for both of them.

Later, getting out of bed was difficult. She felt like she had been on a horse all day. Holden chuckled when she told him, and she retaliated by hitting him over the head with a pillow.

They decided to investigate the small downtown area of Cimarron. They were there, so they might as well. The newlyweds got dressed, then set out to have some breakfast and see the sights. They had worked up quite an appetite.

As they strolled down Main Street looking for a suitable diner, they passed the famous "Cattleman's Bank and Bar," where the cowboys could deposit their money and get refreshments at the same time. It wasn't open yet. Holden and Brya cupped their hands around their eyes so that they could see through the glass. "I'd sure like to know who has done business here, Brya. Maybe they even keep the money that was stolen by famous outlaws," Holden said.

She slapped him on the shoulder. "You're funny, Holden. Yeah, maybe Billy the Kid or Calamity Jane were here." They both laughed and kept walking.

Brya and Holden found a busy diner down the street, after smelling food cooking from one block away. Fried potatoes, sausage, eggs and pancakes sure sounded good. Over breakfast, they talked about their move to Muddy Boggy Creek. Afterwards, they walked for a while and then headed back to their suite to make love again. It came as no surprise that they wanted to do nothing but be together, privately.

Muddy Boggy Creek

Eugenia hugged the newlyweds. "Well, I declare, the two lovebirds are back." Brya looked at Holden and blushed, smoothing her skirt down over her knees, in hopes that her grandma wouldn't be able to tell what they had been up to for three days.

Holden stood proud as a peacock and wore his conquest like a medal.

They cordially spoke with Patch and Eugenia for a while before separating to organize their things. Brya and Holden planned on spending the next two days in Cimarron, and come Tuesday morning, at the crack of dawn, they'd leave in search of their chicken farm.

❦

Brya's delicate hands had never packed up one box of anything before. The staff at the Great House had taken care of that. When she entered Eugenia's kitchen and came face to face with pots and pans, brown packing boxes and tissue paper, she exclaimed, "Grandma, what's all this?"

Eugenia smiled. "I can't see a new bride without kitchen utensils or flatware. Let me show you, dear."

Brya perused the array of wedding gifts. "What's this thing for?" She lifted up a funny looking wood implement with a handle. "It looks like something I'd use to chase away a burglar."

Eugenia laughed. "That's called a mallet. It's used to tenderize meat."

Brya's face turned beet red, realizing that she had a lot to learn. "You must take the kitchen seriously because a man has to eat," said Eugenia. Brya hoped that Holden had a lot of patience. She had never given cooking a minute's thought before because Eusabia had always made the food for the family.

The rest of the afternoon was spent under the tutelage of Eugenia. They covered iron skillets, stainless steel knives, jelly jars, and a variety of utensils. Her grandma taught her to pack carefully so that the items could withstand the knocking around in the back of Holden's pickup truck.

As Brya emptied her closet, the last thing she found was her jar with the five hundred dollars in it. She'd forgotten it was there, just like Patch had told her she would. She blew the dust off the lid and sneezed. The late afternoon heat had made her feel sluggish. She wiped the perspiration off her forehead and tossed the jar in between some clothes, so that it wouldn't break. It was comforting to know she had this money but she'd probably never use it because Holden was going to be very successful.

The next day was just as busy for Brya's husband. By the afternoon, they were organized enough to load up the truck. The wedding gifts ranged from old coins to hand-made quilts, and canned goods to scrub boards. The Hunters, for a surprise, had given them lots of towels and bedding. Now they had everything they needed to begin their new home, except furniture.

Their last evening in Cimarron was spent with both families. Everyone sat on the back porch at Patch and Eugenia's listening to the crickets and smelling the honey-suckle. There had been too much food, as usual.

*

The sun bore down much too early the next morning, which meant that it would be a hot travel day. Brya had to face leaving loved ones once again. As she and Holden pulled away from her grandparents' house, with everyone in tears, she couldn't help but study their faces. They were faces of time, experience, significance and wisdom. These people had played a major role in Brya's life, rescuing her from fate's cruelty. Patch, Eugenia, Maud and Virgil stood like strong oak trees. They promised to be there for the new-lyweds as long as they were able. Holden and Brya didn't speak a word as they drove down the tree-lined street, and they didn't look back. They were completely on their own now. This was exciting to Holden and frightening to Brya.

It would take about two days to reach Muddy Boggy Creek, driving straight through. What if they broke down on the road? They'd heard that there was not much to see on the way, only the flat land and red dirt of Oklahoma. They were told that the rural towns were empty and insignificant, too. One long, straight road and occasionally some small, run-down buildings were all the eye could see. They'd heard that Tulsa and Oklahoma City were filled with black people and Indians but lots of oil was being found there. New wildcatters were arriving every day, digging brand new wells.

"Holden, look at all those oil wells dotting the skyline over there. They look like big, black grasshoppers, bobbing their heads up and down. I've never seen wells being drilled before, but someday I hope I can." Brya batted her eyelashes at her husband.

"That's a far cry from rattlesnake watermelons and chickens, don't you think?"

"But the oil business sounds like a good business to be in. My daddy did a lot of drilling in Texas. He promised to show me a gusher one day, but died before that ever happened. It's fascinating to see how they can pull up all that black liquid from the ground."

"Brya, let's take one step at a time. When I'm dead and gone you can marry some rich oil man and dig all the wells you want."

Brya playfully slapped him on the shoulder. "You're too ornery to die. Besides, we'll drill one together some day."

Holden laughed and shook his head. His eyes squinted against the sun. He knew that he could never give Brya what she deserved but he would do the best he could.

The day was a scorcher, just like they thought it might be, with the sun beating down unmercifully. The cracked earth along the highway looked like it needed a long drink of water. In the distance, wavy grasses were blowing in the breeze.

"Holden, what kind of grass is that over there?" She pointed east.

"That's Indian grass, a prairie grass that grazing cattle eat. These grasses feed hundreds of head," he said. Just then, he swerved to the right as a poky, brown, nine-banded armadillo waddled across the road. With its armor on, it looked like it was going into battle.

"That is just about the ugliest creature I've ever seen, Holden," Brya said.

He agreed. "They look like leftovers from the prehistoric days. But, you know, Brya, they're actually good to eat."

"Oooh, Holden, you're disgusting!" He just loved to tease. "What do those things eat anyway?"

"Snails, insects, earthworms and spiders," he said, "and if you agitate them, they'll roll up in a tight ball so no animal can get through their armor."

Brya kept watching this ancient-looking creature as it crossed the burning highway. Red ants and dust, armadillos and scorpions. Was that *all* she had to look forward to? Burned in her memory were the sad, lean faces of those desperate migrants that she and Patch saw on the way to Cimarron.

❦

After a few rest stops, gasoline, and food, they had traveled into their next day. The scenery remained the same.

As night fell, Muddy Boggy Creek appeared out of nowhere. The wind had grown stronger. The dust was so thin it couldn't be seen in the air, yet it was felt in the lungs.

While entering the outskirts, Holden and Brya found themselves driving through a decaying neighborhood.

"Oh my gosh, Holden, Grandpa was right! This really is nothing like Cimarron. What have we gotten ourselves into?" She grabbed his arm.

"Brya, I'm sure our farm will be better than this. Everything will be all right. I promise." He placed his arm around her shoulder but she pulled away.

Brya swallowed as her husband meandered through the middle of town. The Depression had created deserted stores and shabbily dressed people—some even scarred and disfigured. Refugees, driven from their land, sat lonely and perplexed as the lights of the truck blinded their mournful eyes. Then the night devoured them as if they never existed.

❦

The Pioneer Hotel popped up in front of them, boasting that they had the best chicken feather beds in town. Holden and Brya were very tired and luckily, it looked like a reasonable place to stay.

Holden parked the truck in front of the hotel as a lame passerby stared at the loaded-down vehicle. He eyed it sharply as he dragged his foot along the ground and disappeared into the dark. Brya hoped that her five hundred dollars was safely tucked away. As she stepped down out of the truck, she heard a crunch under her feet. Dead locusts lay on the ground. Smashed ones were smeared on nearby windows. "What do you think happened here?" she grimaced. Things were going from bad to worse, she thought as tears welled up in her eyes.

He shook his head. "I don't know. I'll ask the hotel clerk."

The Pioneer turned out to be one of the oldest hotels in town, clean, and affordable for them. Holden didn't anticipate having to stay there long. With the Depression and all, he hoped to find a small spread outside of town as soon as possible. They walked up to the front desk. A clean-shaven young man with a bright smile turned around and offered his help.

"My wife and I have just driven in from Cimarron and we're very tired. We're looking to buy a chicken farm in the area and need somewhere to stay till we can purchase one. Do you have a large room that we could have for a week, until we get settled?"

"Of course. I have no doubt you'll enjoy your time here, too. You can stay as long as you need to because we're not that busy."

The clerk turned around to get a brass key and some papers for Holden to fill out. Brya wiped some perspiration off her forehead and leaned up against the counter. Her cotton dress stuck to her skin from the heat. Holden slid his fingers through his damp hair as he filled out the forms.

"Excuse me sir," Brya said. "We noticed when we were getting out of our truck that there are dead locusts everywhere. Where did they come from?"

The clerk told them a long story about a locust swarm they had a few days ago. "Suddenly, there was a loud, thundering vibration, which came from the locust wings, and next, a large, black cloud of them came out of nowhere. The swarm was so big that it almost covered the sun. Next thing you knew, the locusts were covering everything." He continued, "If you were driving, your windshield wiper couldn't work fast enough for you to see where you were going. It was dangerous. The tires crunched over thousands of them and made it too slick to drive. I never saw anything like it in my life. My mama told me that they were so bad, they ate the polka dots off my Aunt Milly's kitchen curtains. This swarm didn't stay around long enough to lay more eggs, thank God. As quickly as they came, they went. But they left a lot of damage behind, eating anything and everything in their path. You should be able to pick up a place easily because of what happened. You're lucky you didn't drive in until today."

Holden and Brya were speechless. What if they had driven into that mess?

The hotel room was spacious and comfortable—all they needed for a short stay. They bathed, cleaned up and headed down to a late dinner.

On the way back to the room, Holden bought the *Boggy Creek Times* from the same clerk at the front desk. He was interested in finding out if any farms might be for sale. As they climbed the staircase, Brya stopped to admire an etching of an Indian squaw on horseback. It touched her heart. She knew what it felt like to be a nomad.

Once in the room, Holden sat down on the bed to relax and read. Brya curled up beside him. He looked over the real estate section and came across a couple of good possibilities. Due to the locust invasion, one small farm outside of town had come up for sale. They'd look at it first thing in the morning. And that was the last Brya remembered before falling asleep.

❦

Holden was on the phone bright and early. Brya had just opened her eyes and began stretching when she heard him talking to someone, saying that they'd be there in a couple of hours.

Brya sat up in bed. "What on earth are you doing, honey?" It didn't suit her personality to wake up early, but it looked like they were going to visit a farm that was for sale as soon as they had breakfast.

"The sooner we get cracking, the sooner we'll have a home," Holden said.

He looked at Brya lying in the bed, and leaned over to kiss her and that was all it took—he moved over her and into her like an animal.

❦

They arrived at the farm that Holden was interested in, happy but hungry. It was situated about a mile and a half outside of Muddy Boggy Creek. Nothing was around it at all. Brya could faintly see a lonesome-looking shack in the distance. As much as she loved her husband, he was wrong. This farm didn't look any better than the rest of the town. They drove down a narrow, dusty road to the house, where random holes from snakes and other burrowing critters had been dug in the parched soil. Locusts had swept through here for sure; plant stalks were stripped bare and all the trees were leafless. Not even one leaf was left lying on the ground. Between the Depression and the invasion of the insects, it looked as though these farmers lost everything. Brya started to cry. She was no better off than a migrant, living in whatever she could find. She pulled out a fine french handkerchief that belonged to her mama, which looked so out of place here.

Dead locusts lay on the ground everywhere. An old, broken-down Ford, rusty tricycles, and toys were strewn everywhere. Holden and Brya touched the stately trunk of an old redbud tree that stood by the house. A big truck tire hung from it. They walked up the creaky, unstable steps. Holden knocked but no one answered. He knocked again, and this time they heard footsteps. A tall, rugged woman with lots of thick, red hair opened the door. With hands on her hips, she gave a gracious "Howdy, folks," and asked if they were the Hunter couple she talked to.

Brya looked at this woman in amazement. "Yes, ma'am, we are." She fit Brya's image of Annie Oakley, the famous sharpshooter. Her hair was so high and tangled that birds could have built a nest in it.

She heartily shook hands with the newlyweds. "Hi, I'm Irene Jones. You'll meet my husband Fred in a minute." She escorted them into the small, messy living room. The walls needed painting and the furniture was dirty.

"What kind of farming did you do?" Holden asked.

"We grew corn and some cotton, but the crops didn't pay enough to get us through the Depression and the locusts destroyed whatever crops we had left," Irene replied.

"What are you going to do?" Brya asked.

"We have two children that need to be fed, and the money we get for the farm will hopefully buy us a new life somewhere else. My husband's young enough to work in the oil fields where he heard they're hiring. What do y'all plan on farmin'?" Irene asked.

"We plan to raise chickens and sell eggs from some, but mostly we want to raise them for food," Holden said.

Irene pondered this for a moment and then suggested they take a look at the barn. She said that it just might suit their needs.

They walked through the house, stepping over toys along the way. When they got to the kitchen, Brya almost fainted. All she could see was mildew, dirt and peeling paint. A window located over a sink of dirty dishes faced out onto the back of the farm.

"Would y'all like some water?" Irene asked as she turned on the tap.

"Yes ma'am, it's awfully hot," Brya replied.

They cringed as the pipes shuttered, spewing forth rust-colored water.

"Fred can tell ya how to fix those blasted pipes and your water won't be so funny lookin'," Irene said as she guzzled some of the grotesque liquid. "Besides, if you let it run a while, it gets clear."

Brya shivered.

The Jones' had an old, oversized icebox and a wood-burning stove that would come with the house. The room had limited workspace with a tiny pantry in the corner. There was just enough room to hold a few canned goods, sugar and flour.

Out in the back, nestled in front of an empty field, stood a large, red barn. "It actually looks to be in better shape than the house," Holden whispered.

Brya saw nothing redeeming in it.

Irene yelled for her husband. "Fred, there are some folks here to see ya."

A rickety barn door opened and out came Fred, a middle-aged man who appeared to have the weight of the world on his shoulders. Two dirty children, a boy and a girl, darted out from behind him.

When Fred got to the back door he put out his four-fingered hand to Holden. "Howdy. So, you're here about the farm?" he said wiping the sweat from his brow.

"Yes, we just got married," Holden explained, "and have decided to settle in Boggy Creek to try our luck at chicken farming. We want to sell eggs and fryers to stores and restaurants in the state."

"I hope you have better luck than I had," Fred said, turning away and walking toward the barnyard. He seemed quite eager to get on to the business of selling the place.

The barn was run-down, too, but it seemed to have enough room to begin raising the brooders. Holden could build wooden boxes and put lights on the baby chicks. It would be a perfect place to keep them safe from coyotes, chicken hawks, foxes, and possums.

As Brya glanced around at the barren landscape, she knew that she couldn't live in a place like this for very long. Surely Holden would make lots of money in no time and move to a big, prosperous city where they would raise a big family. Maybe he'd decide to dabble in the oil business after all. She loved her husband, and for now, being there with him was better than being someplace nicer without him.

"This would be a good place for you to begin your business," Fred remarked. "You goin' to raise anything else?"

"I'm intent on raising rattlesnake watermelons," Holden replied.

Fred understood where the young man was coming from. He once had dreams himself.

The Joneses took the Hunters in the farm truck to show what they had in the way of acreage. It all looked like a lot of dirt to Brya. And nothing was growing except her dislike for the place.

Irene and Fred had just found out that the house was about to go into foreclosure and hoped that the newlyweds could purchase it soon.

Holden liked the farm and wanted to buy it. It needed a tremendous amount of work, but he was confident he could do it. After a meager lunch, consisting of stale bread, honey, and tea, the Hunters said good-bye and went back to town. They found the Midwest Bank of Oklahoma, which held the title to the farm, and were directed to the office of Mr. Davenport, who was president of the bank.

His scrutinizing brown eyes peered over his wire-rimmed glasses. "I hear you want to purchase the Jones' farm. What do you plan on doing with it?"

This is where Brya's interest failed her. They had gone over this until she was blue in the face. She distracted herself by staring at the pictures on Mr. Davenport's desk.

Mr. Davenport rubbed his chin as he listened. Brya continued to be in her own world, studying the objects in the office. This kept her from getting any more nervous and jittery than she already was. Actually, the room was kind of sterile. Grandpa Patch's office wasn't much different.

Perspiration began to show through Holden's blue shirt. He was nervous, all right. Mr. Davenport was paying some important attention to him.

It had been about an hour, when out of nowhere Mr. Davenport scratched his bald head, and said, "I've heard of crazier things than raising rattlesnake watermelons and chickens, and it appears to me that you are dependable. You got yourself a deal, Mr. Hunter."

Brya, in a state of confusion, shot up out of her chair and headed for the door.

"Please bear with us, my wife's a little excited." Holden hurriedly shook hands and raced to find her.

Brya was standing on the sidewalk, crying.

He took her by the shoulders, lifting her chin so that he could see her once vibrant eyes. These were not tears of happiness.

"Honey, I know that this run-down farm is not even close to what we had in mind. You deserve better. But we have to start somewhere. Between your resourcefulness and my know-how, we can conquer anything. One day, you and I are going to sit on the porch of our Great House, in awe of where we came from."

Brya just couldn't see it.

Jackrabbit Road

On an overcast September first, two weeks after signing the papers, Brya and Holden checked out of the Pioneer Hotel and headed for their farm.

After they came to an abrupt stop, and the dust had settled, Brya rubbed her eyes and stiffened. The old wooden shack looked even more depressing than before. The junk cars were gone, along with the rusty tricycles. She had dreamed of all kinds of houses before—this was not one of them. Patch and Eugenia's place looked like a palace in comparison.

Geraniums, she thought. Red geraniums. That would brighten things up.

The next few days were spent sweeping out dusty rooms and sneezing incessantly. The young couple scrubbed off crayon drawings that the children had left on the bedroom walls. Tiny cobwebs of spiders hung in corners and had to be knocked down with a broom. Brya never had to clean up anything before. Scrubbing kitchen linoleum took hours of back-breaking work, and lots of elbow grease. No telling how many years of food lay crusted and trapped in the corners. She had a new respect for Eusabia's and Grandma's endeavors. Needless to say, sleep came easily for them on Mama Beatrice's daybed.

Early one morning, as the sun poured through the windows, Brya rolled over to touch her husband but he was gone. She jumped up, threw on her robe and ran to the back porch calling his name. No answer. She dashed straight for the barn, shouting, "Holden!" Again, no answer. Fear ripped through her like a knife.

Holden stuck his head out the barn door and yelled, "I'm cleaning out the barn before it gets too hot. What are you yelling for?"

"Oh, nothing, honey. I just wondered where you were."

Holden was in his overalls. Sprigs of hay were stuck all over his clothing. He was cleaning the barn and raking the floor to make room for his brooder pens and baby chicks.

For Brya, the chicken business was a pain in the neck but her husband took it very seriously. All of that 'to do' about birds, she thought. First, they had to build the pens that would hold the chicks until they were old enough to move outside. When the pens and lights were finished, Holden could order the brooder chicks and leghorns.

"Brya, I plan on ordering a rooster just for you. It'll be your own personal alarm clock and you won't have any excuse not to get up early every morning," Holden told her as he laughed hysterically.

"Holden Hunter, you're not very funny!" She turned and marched back to the house to get ready to leave for Muddy Boggy Creek.

On the outskirts of town, Holden pulled their truck into a Caminol Oil service station and asked for directions to Hanson's Feed Store. They found out that it was about two blocks down from the Pioneer Hotel.

When they walked in, they were struck by the over-whelming smell of alfalfa. It was a heavy, pungent odor, and Brya began sneezing uncontrollably. "Are you all right, sweetheart?"

She nodded. "I need your handkerchief."

The plump, gray-haired clerk looked up from the counter and asked if he could help, but not before spitting his chewing tobacco in a can. Brya was repulsed, just like she was when Miss Grisholm spit the nasty stuff on her leg.

Holden explained about their plans for the old Jones' place and told the clerk they needed chickens and supplies.

The two men decided that about two hundred and fifty chicks would do to start with. Then the old man said, "Are you going to raise these chickens for eggs or meat 'cause chickens don't start giving eggs for about five months, and aren't decent to eat for another two or three months. Think you'll survive till the chicks are old enough to produce?"

Holden and Brya looked at each other in shock. They had overlooked a very important point. How could they support themselves and meet the mortgage payment during an unproductive five months? For a moment, there was silence.

Recognizing their dilemma, the clerk offered a piece of advice: "If I was just starting out, I'd buy thirty or forty of the more mature laying hens and one hundred and fifty female chicks and a rooster. That way, you'll have eggs to sell while your chicks are beginning to develop."

"Great idea," said Holden. "Do you have the laying hens here, and how much do they cost?"

"The hens and rooster are here, but the chicks need to be ordered. They should arrive within the week." After the old man scribbled some figures down, he said that the poultry would run about seventy-five dollars. The price was afford-able.

"What'll we need for supplies and how much will that be?" Holden asked.

"Follow me," the clerk replied.

Near the back of the store, he showed them lumber, chicken wire, electrical fixtures, and chicken feed. All for the price of thirty-five dollars.

After their bill was settled, the clerk reminded them that the chicks would be delivered within the week.

Brya was glad to be leaving the place. Her nose was red and raw from sniffing the alfalfa, and now her eyes were watering, too. Holden shook the clerk's hand and thanked him for all his advice.

As they walked back to their truck, Brya broke down. "My nose runs like a faucet and my eyes water all the time, Holden. I don't think I'm cut out for this farming life."

He extracted the used handkerchief from her hand and gently dabbed her nose. "Getting settled is always the worst part of moving. I've helped friends and neighbors relocate, and all the women go through the same thing. You'll be fine in no time."

She was silent. When? she thought.

Suddenly, Brya glanced up and noticed a Woolworth's five and dime store. This took her mind off her troubles. She tugged on her husband's hand and begged him to go inside. Once there, she made a beeline for the candy counter. In front of her were several large glass jars filled with colorful candies.

Holden grinned. "Brya, you remind me of a little child." She was strong and Holden knew it. In time, he thought things would be more prosperous. For a penny, Brya selected two peppermint sticks, one for each of them to enjoy on their drive home.

They needed to make the most of the afternoon because the delivery order was to arrive at the farm the next day. Brya decided that she needed a break from inhaling the hay and the dust, so she remained in the kitchen, only to agonize over what drawers to put her kitchen utensils in.

Later, as she was making some headway in the kitchen, Holden called for her. When she reached the barn, she could see by the way he was moving that his muscles were sore. They took a break and sat on one of the hay bales to rest. As Brya massaged his back, Holden contemplated the building of his pens and the work he had to accomplish within a week's time.

"Holden, what about the hens? Where will you put them until the pens get built?"

"Well, honey, they'll just have to run loose in the barn. At least they're protected in here."

He got up, stretched a little, and began spreading yellow hay on the barn floor. He piled up an area for a nest so that they could begin laying their eggs. He needed those hens to produce right away.

Brya's nose was starting to run, so she headed back to her kitchen. In an attempt to impress her husband, she decided to make her first big meal—a pot roast. When Holden finally came in for dinner, she was having a miserable time. Water for the vegetables was boiling over, and there was smoke spewing out of the oven. He opened the door slowly to let the thick smoke escape and then reached in to pull out something that was small and burned. Tears streamed down her face. "I ruined our dinner! I know you're hungry and now we don't have anything to eat. I can't cook, let alone bake a pie." She sniffed so hard, she snorted.

Holden tried not to laugh and placed the charred roast down on the countertop, pushing open the screen door to clear the air. He walked over to his wife and held her tight. "You know, sweetheart, I didn't marry you because I thought you'd be a great cook. I married you because I love you." He pushed her damp hair back from her neck and gave her a big kiss. "Besides, one day you'll figure it out like you do everything else, and I'll figure out this farming thing. Why don't we settle down tonight with a butter and strawberry jam sandwich and start new tomorrow?"

Brya smiled as he wiped her tears away. Holden always had a way of making things better.

At dawn, the Hunters were awakened by the sound of a delivery truck. Holden threw on his trousers and wet down his hair, then ran out to meet the delivery man at the front door. Brya followed close behind—she didn't want to miss a thing. The trucker wanted to know where to set the stuff down, and Holden directed him to the barn.

The man wrinkled his brow and his nose, and with a surly look turned around to leave, mumbling something to himself. "Must not be having a good day," thought Brya. The hens were probably too noisy for him.

The first thing the two men did was put all the hens and the feed in the barn. The hens scurried around, trying to get used to their new location. Holden shut the barn door, leaving them alone to find their way. Next came the supplies. He had ordered enough building material to build the coop, the nesting boxes, and the surrounding pen. He told the grumpy delivery man to stack the supplies against the side of the barn.

As the old coot ambled his way back to the truck, he pulled his underwear from between his cheeks. He thought no one was looking, then yelled back, "What ya want done with this here rooster?" Holden pointed to a shady spot near a birch tree and told him to just set it down there.

"This is one fired-up bird. Be careful or he might just claw his way through your clothes," the trucker said. Brya couldn't believe that a rooster could do that to anyone. Holden thanked him for his advice and agreed that he had seen them get pretty nasty.

Holden went inside to see what his bride was up to. She was pretty proud of herself having conquered some cinnamon toast and coffee. Holden could have cut the coffee with a knife, but knew better than to say a word.

"Brya, after your chores are done, why don't you come out and look at our rooster and the forty hens we now own?" With that, he left to work on the barn.

"In a while, honey."

Holden must have gotten so engrossed in his work he forgot he told his wife to come out and get acquainted with the new rooster.

"Come here, nice rooster," Brya said, casually walking up to it.

Before she knew it, the critter began to come after her, and chased her across the barnyard. She began swatting at it but it attached itself to her dress and wouldn't let go.

"Holden, get this thing off me!" she screamed, swatting at the feathered creature over and over.

He came dashing out of the barn and saw that the rooster had ripped a big hole in Brya's dress. With some effort, he shooed the beast away while trying to quiet his wife.

"Why didn't you tell me he was so mean?" With that, Brya ran into the house, scared and upset, and refused to speak to her husband.

When Holden found Brya, she was curled up pouting on her Mama's daybed in their bedroom. He cautiously walked over and sat down by her.

"Honey, I had no idea that you would go near the new rooster without me being there."

"I didn't know he was so mean. I thought I'd just go over and pet him." Brya reached down and pulled her dress aside, exposing her first battle scar.

He rubbed her head with his chapped hands and begged her forgiveness.

They did all their making up in bed.

The week went by quickly. Holden finished the pen, the coop, and the nesting boxes. Once the laying hens were moved outside, he had one day to build the homes for the baby chicks.

In seven days of back-breaking work, the Hunters created their first working farm. Brya found ways to dodge the rooster. She was beginning to like picking up eggs from the hens in the morning, and then counting them, even though the hay bothered her. The hens hadn't suffered in their move, and Brya was able to collect several dozen eggs the first day. They had a cold cellar where she kept the eggs chilled until the trucker came at the end of the week. Holden sold them to a local grocer in Boggy Creek. After Brya finished gathering eggs, she would head into the barn to see the baby chicks, and even though she knew she shouldn't pick them up, she did anyway. She would hold them in her hands or next to her cheek, feeling the pulse of their tiny, rhythmic hearts. It was just like holding a baby.

Fall was settling in on Muddy Boggy Creek, along with the shiver of coming winter. This year, because of the locust swarm, the surrounding trees didn't create a colorful backdrop to the farm. The rabbits, oddly enough, were still playing games with one another outside. Those games were usually saved for spring. This was Brya's favorite time of year, because it reminded her of the long walks that she and Holden used to take when they first met. As she glanced out of the window watching her husband work, she longed to take those walks again, but he was too busy to stop. She ached for companionship; the babbling radio could entertain her only to a point.

Brya found a small Methodist church near town and began attending the services to try and meet some folks. She was not really a strong, churchgoing individual but at least she was communing with the Lord, and she hoped the Lord in turn would help her meet some nice women. She needed friends badly.

One warm fall day, Brya decided to go to a bake sale that was being held at the church. She put on her sunbonnet that she used for the garden. When Holden dropped her off at church, she could smell the pies. Inside, several women were standing behind booths. In front of them sat every pie imaginable: cherry, pecan, apple, chocolate, and lemon. Brya chatted with everyone she met. Her mama always said that it was the women she needed to talk to; they were the ones that allowed you in the house, not the men. This was hard for Brya because she liked men more than women. They weren't as catty. But she knew she had better listen to the wise words of her mama, who was smart on these social things.

It was here that Brya met Corabelle Lee, her neighbor, and as it turned out, she and her husband Bud owned the land just east of theirs. A farm woman, born and bred, Corabelle Lee knew nothing about the extravagant life Brya came from.

Brya figured that Corabelle could teach her a lot about cooking. She probably weighed three-hundred pounds, with a full, round face the color of ripe cherries. Her tanned hands were the size of a man's.

Brya was right. Corabelle's expertise was good food, and the two women became fast friends. The large woman was always in fine humor and a joy to be around. She would come over maybe twice a week with some recipes and teach Brya how to prepare them. So far, Brya's favorite was Corabelle's grits and cheese. Needless to say, Holden was in love with the new neighbor that could cook.

When Brya wasn't learning to cook, she would attack the housecleaning and wash their clothes—by hand. It was tedious work to haul water from the well in the back, heat it on the stove, then stir the clothes with a large wooden spoon. She had to do it that way, in order for the laundry to get cleaned and disinfected.

She learned to make soap from lye, but it was ruining her hands. They couldn't afford to buy fancy soaps at the store yet. Brya accepted that she was having a hard time with daily chores. She hadn't been raised to do this work, and as far as she was concerned, it was slave labor.

Holden felt sorry for her. He knew there wouldn't be enough money for quite awhile to provide some of the luxuries that she deserved. When he had a few moments to spare, he'd come into the house and give his wife some extra attention.

In Brya's rare spare moments, she would call her grandparents on the telephone or write to her brothers and sisters to let them know about her new life. She hoped they would write her back soon.

One morning, after having a large breakfast, Holden and Brya went over their household records. The hens were doing a fine job of producing eggs, and the money was coming in, slowly but surely.

"Dearest," Brya asked, "do you think we can buy a table and some chairs for the kitchen? I'm tired of sitting on old crates for our meals."

Brya had a winsome way about her and he couldn't turn her down, but he came back with a teasing remark. "You can have what you want as long as you don't try to buy out the store. We'll shop at the Salvation Army and order the rest of the items from the Sears Catalogue." This was a far cry from the French antiques she had grown up around. But Brya was grateful. They were coming up in the world. She threw her arms around his neck, and then ran up to the bedroom to get dressed. When she got upstairs, she felt queasy but figured the fatty bacon had given her indigestion, so she ignored the strange sensation and put her clothes on.

The road was always bumpy on the drive into town, and by this time, Brya's stomach wouldn't let up on her. She rubbed her belly and complained. Holden thought that the excitement was getting the best of her.

In the window of the furniture store stood a maple kitchen table with four straight-backed chairs. It was perfect. Lucky for them, the owner was having a fall clearance. The entire set cost thirty-five dollars.

That evening, Brya's stomach continued to get the best of her but she managed to make a candlelight dinner for the two of them. Holden ate like a horse, scraping his plate clean after finishing off some pork ribs and vegetables. She could only pick at her food.

"Why aren't you eating?"

"I don't feel very good. Maybe I picked up a bug or something." Brya got up from the table and sat on his lap. She gave him a tender kiss and snuggled in his chest.

"I'll do the dinner dishes for you, Brya. Get into bed and rest. I'll be up shortly to keep you company."

She disappeared upstairs to take a bath, but it didn't help. Finally, she crawled into bed, curled up in a ball and drifted off to sleep. She never heard her husband come in.

Sunrise brought the same symptoms. This time, Brya was making frequent trips to the outhouse and throwing up what little breakfast she had. Holden was worried now. He recollected seeing a sign for a doctor on the edge of town, so he telephoned the operator to give him the number.

Holden helped Brya put her clothes on and walked her to the truck. She was pale and weak.

Dr. Brian Bennett was able to see Brya in his office almost immediately, but Holden had to remain in the waiting room.

The doctor gave Brya her first female examination. He didn't find anything wrong, but when he was through poking and prodding, she felt like there was. And going to the bathroom in a cup was disgustingly hard to do. After this degradation, Dr. Bennett took her blood and ran other tests, not speaking two words to her the entire time.

When he was finished, he excused himself, and returned with Holden. Much to Brya's surprise, the doctor had a smile on his face.

"There's a strong chance you're pregnant, Brya. I've given you a pregnancy test," the doctor said, pushing back a shock of white hair that fell on his forehead.

Holden's jaw fell open. He ran his hands through his hair and stuttered, "Doctor, how can you tell if she is or isn't?" A helpless look came over his face.

"We inject the urine into a rabbit and then wait to see whether or not it dies."

"Well, I'll be darned."

Holden and the doctor were talking like Brya wasn't in the room, so she cleared her throat and interrupted. "How long will it take to get the results?"

"The process will take about a week, and my office will call to give you the news." The doctor shook Holden's hand and left the room.

As Brya buttoned the top of her blouse, she and Holden looked at each other in amazement. They had to wait to find out the news—a whole week.

At first, it was a long, silent drive home. Then Holden, without warning, said, "If you're pregnant, I'll be the happiest man in the world." With that, Brya let loose all her emotions. She was thrilled about the possibility of creating a family, and overwhelmed with the thought of Holden loving a baby, just like her daddy did. Now, all of her dreams would come true.

As they pulled into the driveway, reality hit and she remembered all the chores she must do. This wasn't how she planned it. She wanted to be pampered and taken care of, just like she was as a child with Mama Beatrice and Eusabia there to help her.

The next week was the longest week of their lives, especially for Brya. She woke up every day and headed for the outhouse, growing sick and tired of putting her head over the smelly hole on a daily basis. Performing her regular duties was agonizing. Of all the weeks, she saw field mice scampering through the pantry, and then gagged when she saw their droppings. Holden, her hero, would come to dispose of them.

It was awful waiting. What if she wasn't pregnant and had some dread disease? What if she were dying?

No sooner had these questions started swirling through her brain than the phone rang.

"I'm going to be a mother!" she shouted.

Brya dropped the phone and ran outside to tell Holden. Ecstatic, he left all that he was doing to be with her. They sat on the front porch in easy chairs and relished the thought of a little one entering their lives.

By then, maybe the farm would be more prosperous than it was now. Holden felt secure about his ability to run a business, even though the Depression was getting worse and people were standing in bread lines across the country to get food. Money was tight, but food was always on their table, and Brya didn't complain.

They spent Thanksgiving alone on the farm. They wanted to have their family come visit but there wasn't enough furniture to seat everyone, nor beds for them to sleep. Besides, with winter setting in, they couldn't leave the chickens.

Holden and Brya telephoned Patch and Eugenia, who were tickled pink about the news. Holden's parents, just as excited, promised to come for the birth. About the same time, Megan called, and heard the good news as well. She vowed to come visit for Christmas. This lifted Brya's spirits because she had been feeling very isolated.

Holden was even more sexually attracted to his wife now that she was carrying his child. He would come in the house, sometimes as much as three times in one day, to make love. Using new positions, he would slip in and out of her gently and easily, bringing her to new heights of sensation. And she enjoyed learning new ways to satisfy him.

On some cold mornings before her husband was awake, Brya would slide under the covers and manipulate his soft, warm flesh in her mouth until he exploded. Then he would pull her up to him, kissing her face and neck and caressing her body like never before.

Holden's greatest gift to her was the art of unbridled lovemaking.

～

Their lives changed from day to day. Even though the pregnancy was going along well, Brya's emotions swayed back and forth. She was too tired to enjoy the beauty of anything because she felt fat and ugly.

"I never look pretty anymore," became her constant complaint as she stared at her round silhouette in the mirror. At night, when she was alone with her thoughts, she would dream of a beautiful baby, a flat belly, and exquisite clothes.

The young couple added what furniture they could afford, some secondhand. Their home was becoming a cozy nest.

Night after night, Holden's hands traveled her body, exploring the womb that held his baby. He could feel the tiny thump . . . thump . . . thump of its heart. They lay awake for hours, contemplating names to call him or her. So far, nothing seemed appealing.

By Christmas, they had added enough furniture to have both sets of grandparents visit. Megan showed up as well. Their cars carved deep tracks in the snow as they made their way to the plain brown house in the middle of nowhere. Meager red ribbon around porch posts transformed them into candy canes. In the living room sat a three-tiered tumbleweed tree covered with red flannel bows and strings of popcorn.

The folks made a fuss over Brya's belly, which had blossomed in four months' time. They brought presents for the house, including an oak crib and a rocker, packages of handmade baby clothes, cloth diapers, and diaper pins. Apple cider in a jug chilled in the snow for Christmas day, and fresh pies sat on the sideboard.

For Brya, it was wonderful to have her family around and be coddled and pampered once again. She had missed her grandmother's cooking: lumpy mashed potatoes and cornbread dressing, raspberry cobbler and vanilla wafer pudding. Poor Eugenia still suffered from gout, and everyone else, except Megan, complained of new aches and pains.

After Christmas, winter set in hard and furious. It was a good thing that the poultry could be brought into the warm barn. Other farmers weren't that fortunate.

One evening, as the snow fluttered down, Holden and Brya were listening to country and western music on the radio. Suddenly the program was interrupted by a special bulletin. Franklin D. Roosevelt, the new Democratic president, not even sworn in yet, had had an assassination attempt on his life. He escaped injury, but the gun shots killed the mayor of Chicago. What was happening to their fine country?

After the assassination attempt, another bank panic began. Farmers couldn't pay their mortgages. People hurried to their banks to get gold and cash, and this shut down banks everywhere. Then on March 6, 1933, two months before their baby was due, President Roosevelt declared a "bank holiday," and shut down every bank in the United States.

"Holden, come in here," Brya screamed towards the barn, "there's horrible news on the radio!"

Holden flew in the back door, "What on God's earth is wrong?"

"They've closed all the banks in the country! What are we to do? We're going to die just like my daddy did because we won't have any money!"

Holden, stunned, drove into town to get the newspaper. An hour later he returned. She was right.

"Brya, why don't we call Patch to see what he says? Sit down in an easy chair. I don't want you getting so upset. You might hurt yourself or the baby."

"I don't care. I'm so big and miserable Holden, all I want to do is have this child in peace. Everything's wearing me out—the chores, the cooking, this old house. Look at my hands, they're covered with calluses. I'm just not pretty anymore! It's just too much, too much, and now this!"

Holden panics and dials up Patch as fast as he can. "Patch, I'm sorry to bother you, but Brya is hysterical with the banks closing and all. Would you please tell us what's happening?"

"Put her on the phone, son. I'm concerned about her delicate condition."

Holden placed the receiver in Brya's trembling hand.

"Grandpa, I'm so scared."

"Brya, I know this is a drastic measure for the president to take, but in the end, it'll be better for all of us. They're sending special agents to review the books of all the banks, and the ones that aren't in trouble can reopen in about a month. My bank is solvent. I also checked on yours, because I was afraid you'd have a reaction to the news. Don't worry, sweetheart. You and Holden will be fine."

By the time she finally said good-bye to Patch, her trembling had subsided. "Grandpa says that things should be fine in about a month. He's sending us some extra money for any expenses we might have until this blows over. He doesn't want me to use my five hundred dollars, yet."

Holden and Brya had planned to fix up the baby's room during the last couple of months of Brya's pregnancy. She welcomed the distraction. The money from Patch made life easier. They decorated, ate lots of eggs, and waited for the moment when money would free up again. They painted the baby's room blue because it was going to be a boy. Holden said so. The crib was lined with soft bunting and warm blankets. Brya felt healthy and strong as her time approached.

Within a month, their bank had reopened, as did Patch's. But many banks never did. The president's move had ended the crisis, and confidence was restored.

❦

The labor pains started out deep and long. Brya had been picking up some of Holden's clothes in the bedroom when they gripped her lower belly. Suddenly, she was doubled up in pain. She slowly made her way to the back kitchen door and yelled for her husband. He came running.

"I think it's time to go to the hospital," Brya calmly said. Holden ran around like a chicken with its head cut off until he found his keys. Then he put a blanket around her and carried her to the truck. No one had told Brya to pack an overnight bag for her and the baby. The severe pain came and went. Holden pressed hard on the accelerator, but the drive to the hospital seemed to take an eternity.

"Help! Help!" Holden shouted as they drove up to the hospital curb. Brya was immediately whisked away, and he was told to go wait in the lobby.

The shooting pains in her stomach were unbearable as she was wheeled into a room of unfamiliar faces. Voices and faces became blurred. "Holden!" she cried out. "Holden!" No one listened. Brya screamed in pain until finally some shot numbed her lower body and she felt nothing. Dr. Bennett and his team worked feverishly on her; everyone seemed worried. Brya didn't hear any crying, in fact, she didn't hear anything at all. Silence filled the room.

"I'm sorry," Dr. Bennett said as he looked into her bewildered face, gently wiping her wet forehead.

"I want to see my baby, where's my baby?"

"I'm so sorry, Brya. You've given birth to twin boys, and they didn't survive."

Suddenly the hospital room became a blur, and the nearby voices became distant. Dr. Bennett brought Holden into the room and explained to him what had happened. He couldn't speak and looked over at his wife lying on the white, blood-stained table. The tiny bodies of their baby boys had already been removed.

"Dr. Bennett won't let me see them." She cried uncontrollably as Holden held her in his arms. They would never be able to see their sons' faces, only those that they created in their minds. They would never be able to hold them close, or feel their soft, newborn skin, and they would never play with them, or say their names. These tiny beings would become faceless, nameless ghosts floating in the caverns of their minds forever. Tears fell from Holden's eyes and his body shook with sobs. The doctor left them alone. Brya had been sedated just enough so that the edges of the pain were fuzzy.

After a while, they moved her to a hospital bed and took her to room 204—next to a young Cherokee squaw. A white sheet divided them. Holden pulled himself together to try and console his wife, but all she could do was stare at the ceiling. He bent down to kiss her, pushing her damp hair back. She couldn't move a muscle, or even acknowledge her husband. She couldn't imagine his pain because her world had been shattered. She turned and looked at him sitting on the cold floor, disturbed, not understanding what to do. His head was buried in his hands.

"My babies, my babies," she said faintly. Holden got up off of the floor, took her hand and looked down, trying to get her to speak.

She slowly turned toward him, "I've lost my family again. Why can't anything live that's around me?" Brya turned away from her husband and started crying.

"This isn't your fault. It could have happened to anyone," Holden said.

In her drug-induced fog, Brya remembered Eusabia telling her to pat her shoulder and a guardian angel would take care of her.

"Holden, if only I'd listened to Eusabia and patted my shoulder, our guardian angel would have protected us from this nightmare." She slowly raised her hand to her shoulder. "I took it for granted that our baby would be fine. What have I done?"

All through the night, Holden sat on the bed and rocked her, listening to the melancholy chant of the Cherokee woman, who was lamenting her own losses.

The next few days were bleak as Brya's moods spiraled up and down. On one hand, she cursed the death of her two sons, and on the other, she wondered how she could ever have taken care of two. Then she felt guilty for having thoughts like that, and became hysterical again. Holden sat and listened, trying to deal with her pain.

Because she was so depressed, the doctor kept her in the hospital a little longer. While there, the funeral of her boys took place. After seeing the death of her parents, it was just too much to have to bury two more family members. The service was held at Brya's church, and both sets of grandparents were there. She heard it was a short service. What does one say to two babies that didn't have a chance in this life?

Shortly after returning home from the hospital, Holden closed the babies' room off from the rest of the house so Brya wouldn't look in.

But that didn't stop the nightmares and the loneliness from invading her soul.

Late one night, Holden was startled by his wife's screaming. "Daddy, no! Mama, don't leave me!"

"Brya, wake up," Holden said, gathering her trembling body in his arms. "It's all right, I'm here."

"Oh Holden, that was an awful dream; Mama, Daddy, the gunshot, my babies . . . I kept falling into a pit and I couldn't get out."

"You're not down there, Brya, you're here with me." He stroked her head softly, wondering how to ease her suffering.

"I haven't had one of those nightmares since my parents died. I've had bad dreams before, but I kept thinking that they wouldn't come back."

Holden had lost his younger brother in a farming accident, and he knew from experience that pain didn't die.

Brya smiled sleepily and snuggled close. "As long as I'm in your arms, I'll feel safe, and those horrible dreams won't be able to hurt me."

"I'll always be here to love you, Brya. You mean the world to me."

Holden got a twinkle in his eye remembering what the doctor had said.

"You know, sweetheart, Dr. Bennett said that the best recovery you could have would be to try and make a baby again." Brya felt a familiar tingle in her abdomen. It had been a long time.

During the next few months, Holden was inside of her over and over again. Orgasm after orgasm. It wasn't long before her belly was ripe with his seed again.

PART II: *Olivia Hunter*

Birth and Death

On March 2, 1934, Olivia Hunter was born, but not easily. The doctor told Holden that Brya had a fifty-fifty chance of surviving.

Weighing in at ten pounds, the baby was bigger than the twin boys were together. During the birth, Brya's insides hemorrhaged and the doctor had to perform an emergency hysterectomy. It took several days for Brya to come around.

When she awakened, Holden and the doctor were staring down on her. She didn't know what day it was.

"Hi, sweetheart. It's me, Holden."

"Hello, Brya," the doctor said.

She slowly reached out her hand to her husband's and gave a gentle squeeze. He bent down and kissed her on the forehead.

"How are you feeling?" said the doctor.

"Drained and stiff, Dr. Bennett. I'm so groggy. What's happened to me?"

The doctor sat on the edge of the bed. "Brya, you have a beautiful baby girl who is just fine, but you had some complications." She didn't say a word. "We had to perform a hysterectomy in order to save your life. Holden already knows about it. Birthing the baby tore your insides so badly that we had no choice. You won't be able to have any more children."

Holden had a frightened look in his eye. Brya could tell that he was beside himself and it was hard for him to hold back his emotion.

The doctor excused himself. "Brya, when you want to talk more about it, I'll come back." Holden took his place on the bed, not letting go of his wife's hand.

"I've been so scared for you, but you're going to be okay," he said with tears in his eyes. "You mean more to me than anything in this world, and I couldn't bear the thought of losing you."

"Oh, Holden." She ran her hand through his hair. "Nothing's going to happen to me, and besides, we have a beautiful daughter that I can't wait to hold. I'll spring back in no time, you'll see." Her words seemed to help him.

"The grandparents are all here," Holden said, trying to bring a little more happiness to the conversation. "They've seen the baby through the windows in the nursery. The staff won't let us in there, and I'm upset. I want to hold our little girl."

"What does she look like?" Brya asked.

"She looks like a cherub, honey, with olive skin, dark brown hair, and rosy cheeks. Actually, she looks a lot like me." Now she knew she had her husband back.

Brya wouldn't ever forget this moment of having her husband not only concerned, but grateful for what she had accomplished. She had never been happier to be alive.

"What are the grandparents up to today?" Brya asked.

"They're at the house taking care of me and the farm. We're waiting for you to get well and come home. I don't think I've ever eaten so much in my life." They both laughed.

"Holden, will you send for the doctor, please?"

He suddenly turned somber. "What's the matter, are you all right?"

"Of course, silly. I just have a few questions, that's all."

It wasn't long before the doctor returned.

"How long will it take for me to recuperate?"

"You've had major surgery, Brya, but you're tough. I suspect that you'll be in here about three weeks. In fact, your baby might go home before you do. With all those grandparents, your child will be in good hands."

She didn't mind having to stay that long in the hospital, especially as sore as she was. She just felt sorry for her husband. With so much coming and going, he wasn't able to tend to his chores.

Finally, the doctor allowed them to hold their daughter for the first time. Brya had tried so desperately to have a baby, and now her very own child was in her arms. The doctor had Holden put on a surgical gown and mask, and he looked as though he was ready to operate. As soon as Olivia was placed in his arms, he bonded to her. Brya could only see his eyes, but deep love poured out of them.

◈

As Brya started to feel better, her reaction to the hysterectomy was surprising. She was slowly beginning to feel strong now—and she had one healthy child. It didn't bother her that she couldn't birth another. Everything she'd always wanted was right here. Nothing would separate her from her family again. Nothing. She was starting to feel confident.

Brya was a new woman by the time she left the hospital. As Holden helped her into the truck, he told her, "You are more beautiful than ever, Brya, and now I'm headed home to live with my two incredible women."

Knowing that privacy was important for a new family, the grandparents decided to relocate to the Pioneer Hotel. Patch appreciated all of Holden's efforts but it was extremely hard to see his granddaughter live like this. He would keep his silence. It would take about six more weeks for

Brya to recover, and as soon as she was back on her feet, their job would be over.

Looking at their farm for the first time in a while made Brya depressed, even though she was happy to be alive. As she stepped out of the pickup truck onto Hunter soil, she sniffed the fresh air and clutched her baby to her aching breasts. Due to the surgery, she was unable to breast-feed but they were still full of milk. It was a messy process.

The hens were busy at work, and the rooster was spouting off, as usual. A stray calico cat dashed across the dirt. This was not the special home she had envisioned for her baby.

As she approached the front steps, she kicked over a glass milk bottle by accident, spilling the cream and all its contents on the porch.

"Forgive me. I suppose I'm a nervous mother."

"Don't worry about it, that stray cat will be back in no time flat to lick it up. I'll get the milkman here as soon as possible." Brya looked at Holden's face and noticed how tired and drained he looked. This whole episode had been a strain on him, too. He was always there for her, no matter what.

It was a sunny spring day. There was ample food in the refrigerator and baby presents from the grandparents in the kitchen. The laundry was done, and the bedding was fresh. The baby's room was full of light and smelled clean. It no longer needed to stay sealed like a tomb.

A note from Corabelle tacked to the front door said she couldn't wait to see Olivia. What a true friend she was.

Brya loved the feeling of a big family. Joy and excitement filled the house. Only when she held her first great-grandchild did Eugenia stop bustling about. Her aged fingers stroked the baby's soft, fuzzy head. She catered to her great granddaughter's every whim.

Despite popular opinion, Patch would bundle Olivia up in warm blankets and take her on the porch for private chats. He'd tell her about the world and give her business advice. She had captured his heart.

Maud refused to return to the hotel at night. Like a tireless workhorse, she would feed the little bundle of joy during the wee hours of the morning, while the new mother got her rest.

Virgil tried to copy Patch. He would sneak off with Olivia to show her farming equipment. This way, if something broke, she could fix it. However, Maud wasn't happy with his disappearing act, and she spared no words. Virgil had to tow the line and stay put.

Olivia was a good baby. All she did was eat and sleep. It didn't take her long to know who her mama and daddy were. Her hair color stayed a soft brown but her eyes turned a pale forest green. The look was quite a striking contrast to her olive skin.

Holden and Brya were having a terrible time with diapers and diaper smell. Brya's grandmother showed her how to clean and sterilize them in boiling pots of water on the outside burners. The young couple were beginning to understand that babies and diapers were arduous work.

❦

One morning, as Brya knelt and wiped up some Pablum off the shiny kitchen floor, the phone rang.

"Brya, it's Megan. How are you doing, little mother?"

"Megan!" she yelled, dropping her cloth full of baby food on the floor, "I'm doing fine, just a little sore inside, but getting better. How are *you*, sis?"

"I want to come visit for a couple of days, see the baby, and tell you some exciting news."

"Oh Megan, I'd love to see you. The grandparents just left and we'll have plenty of time to ourselves, just talking and catching up. Get here as soon as you can. We'll be waiting!"

As Brya hung up the telephone, she looked down at her baby and said, "Olivia Hunter, your Aunt Megan is coming. She'll not let you out of her sight, I'm sure."

Olivia just grinned a little as her mother adjusted the pacifier that was dangling out of her cute rosebud lips. Just then, Holden came in from the barn. "Megan's coming to visit, sweetheart."

"Great." He sat down in the chair to rest. "Some relatives you can live without, but she's a blessing." The sound of thunder rolled far in the distance.

Holden seemed content now that his wife was home. He could tend to his barnyard work, and not have to worry about other things. The farm was doing well. The hens were expert egg layers, and another batch of baby chicks were growing by leaps and bounds. Finally, Holden and Brya had gotten a little bit ahead. In about a year, Holden hoped to plant his bumper crop of rattlesnake watermelons. By then, he thought he could hire someone to help him. While Brya was in the hospital, he met a few of the neighbors, including Corabelle's husband, Bud. They hit it off right away. The young couple were slowly settling into the ways of Muddy Boggy Creek.

Sometimes, humid weather made Holden as thirsty as if it were a very hot day, and he would come in and get lots of water. One afternoon, Brya happened to be standing at the sink, washing dishes. Her husband wanted her badly, but the doctor said that it would be several weeks before it was safe to have sexual relations. The urge to be near him was strong on her part, too. Brya told him to sit at the kitchen table facing out, and she would be back shortly. When she returned from putting the baby to sleep, she was naked. Childbearing hadn't damaged her body one bit—no stretch marks, and her skin was as smooth as silk. She chose to ignore the long scar across her stomach. Brya turned some romantic music on the radio and slowly walked over to Holden, placing a soft, full breast in his mouth. His hands softly kneaded them as he kissed her. He devoured her chest and belly like a ravenous wild animal as she undulated in front of him. Then, she bent down and unzipped his work pants and reached in. It wasn't long before he exploded in her mouth. She ached to have him inside of her but would have to wait a while longer.

Megan was so excited to see Olivia that she forgot to hug her sister or Holden. She grabbed her niece and swirled her around. "You are so exquisite, Olivia, and our parents would be so proud of you."

That was the first time Brya had consciously thought about her parents in a long while. Even her bad dreams had subsided. "Olivia would have been the apple of their eye, I'm sure."

Megan gaped at the dismal surroundings.

Brya picked up on her sister's reaction. "Oh Megan, this is just temporary until we raise enough money to live grand again."

Megan was used to her sister's lofty ambitions but hoped, for Brya's sake, that she was right. As she was led into the house, she cringed. The inside was not much better. Compared to the Great House, this was a hovel.

Holden left to buy some supplies in town and Megan settled into being Auntie Megan and fed Olivia her bottle. Brya was appreciative of the gesture because her feet and back were always weary. After the baby had some time to get well-acquainted with her aunt, they tucked her in tightly for a nap and the two sisters flopped on the sofa to begin their non-stop talking.

"Brock's working hard as a roughneck in Venezuela's oil fields but I don't know when he'll return," Megan said. "Emilia will finally get her wish to be on the concert tour. And no one's heard from Duke, which doesn't surprise me. No telling what's happened to him and that worries me." Megan had a motherly way of staying in touch with her brothers and sisters, so she knew the latest news. Brya occasionally wrote to them, but it was difficult. Each time she wrote it brought up painful memories of that horrible day for her. Besides, she seldom got a reply.

"I have some incredible news," Megan announced.

"Tell me, tell me!" Brya said, as she licked her fingers and handed Megan a piece of chocolate pudding cake, fresh from the oven.

"I've met a wonderful man who lives in California. And I've decided to marry him and move there."

Brya dropped her fork on the floor. "You what?" she said. "My baby sister's moving lock, stock, and barrel to California? I won't get to be near you anymore. Tell me where you met this love of your life."

Megan blushed. "Well, my friend Ann Connors was giving a small party at her house for a friend of hers, and James happened to be visiting family and came over to the party with them. That's his name, James Cooper. Anyway, he couldn't take his eyes off me and I just knew I was going to marry him. We struck up a conversation at the table, and the next thing I knew, he extended his trip."

Brya felt delighted and melancholy at the same time. As she recovered from the startling news, she began talking about visiting Megan. They could bring all of their babies to the seashore in California.

Megan placed her dessert plate on the coffee table and dreamily fell against the back of the sofa. "I'm so in love, sis."

"Where does he live, Megan? And what does he look like?"

"James has a small farm in the San Fernando Valley. And he's, well, so . . . masculine. His dark eyes look right through you. His thick, brown hair is bleached from the sun. He swears that California's the place everyone's moving to now—it's so prosperous and modern. We'll be living right near Hollywood, where all those rich and famous movie stars live. Bring Olivia, come to the beach, see the movie stars, and get autographs."

Brya finally got caught up in her sister's excitement. It sounded like a fun place to visit, and she knew that Olivia would love the beach and the surf playing at her feet.

"Oh, Megan, I'm thrilled for you, but I'll miss you terribly."

"I plan on keeping in close touch with everybody. So never fear, Brya. You'll probably hear from me even more than you do now."

They carried on all afternoon until they heard the hungry cry of the baby. Megan's tireless energy wouldn't let Brya do anything while she was there. She said she was getting in practice for when she had her own little ones.

The few days that Megan stayed at the farm were filled with fun and laughter. Brya was sad to see her go but comforted herself with the idea that she would now have a larger extended family—and trips to California, an escape from Muddy Boggy Creek.

Holden was working harder than ever. He was trying to figure out a way to set up his new crops. He felt more pressure than ever to perform for his family. But he made time to play with his daughter, to rock and to soothe her, and he made sure he let his wife know how much he cared.

Olivia was a hearty child. She ate well and rarely got fussy. It made her giggle to watch the chickens talk to one another. Every time she saw the infamous rooster, her eyes widened. At an early age, she expressed a smart fear of the feathery beast.

Summer brought out the child in Holden. The garden hose became his toy and Brya couldn't relax for a minute. She constantly had to look over her shoulder, especially when she was hanging up the clothes to dry. It started with one squirt, then it didn't matter anymore.

Early one morning, before the sun came up, Brya heard her husband coughing and sneezing in the bathroom. Strange. He was never sick.

"Honey," Brya said, rising sleepily out of the sheets, "are you all right?"

"I'm fine. I just picked up a cold." He blew his nose and walked away.

"I'll go make you some hot tea, sweetheart," she yelled. "It won't take me very long." Brya got out of bed and stepped into her slippers.

The kettle was whistling loudly when Holden entered the kitchen. The morning light filtered through the curtains throwing a pale, orange cast around the room. He sat down with a thud and complained that he hadn't ever had a cold like this one before. He felt achy and tired. He clasped his hands around the teacup and breathed the fumes. Brya handed him a jar of clover honey and a slice of lemon.

She took a long look at her handsome husband and noticed that the bottom of his nose was red and swollen and his eyes appeared dark and sunken. "Why don't you rest today, Holden? I'll take care of the hens, collect the eggs, and clean up. You never rest."

But he was adamant about staying busy. "If I don't, I'll go crazy."

Holden put the cup down and ignored his breakfast, "I'm not that hungry now, maybe I'll eat later." He slowly got up from the chair, rubbed the back of his aching neck, and walked out to the backyard, pestering ole Henry the rooster. About that time, Olivia woke up, and a new workday began.

As summer turned to fall, Holden couldn't seem to get rid of the cough. He went to see Dr. Bennett, who told him that it was just a bad season for colds and all—so hot, humid, and dusty. The doctor gave him a cough medicine that tasted like bitter cherries and told him to try and take it easy.

Holden arrived home from the doctor's fatigued. He wanted more than anything to play with his daughter but just didn't have the energy. For the first time in his life, he took a nap in the middle of the day. Brya sat alone in the living room and played with Olivia. Holden had never been like this before. It felt lonely not to have him around to pester and pinch her. He would be better, she told herself. It was just a silly cold.

But his condition worsened. By September's end, the persistent cough increased and Holden's ability to work long hours diminished. He had fevers that came and went, nausea, and unexplainable rashes. Before he got sick, he had taught his wife how to drive. Out of necessity, she drove him to the doctor, and it was there she learned the startling news. Holden had contracted tuberculosis and it was in an advanced stage.

Brya demanded to speak to Dr. Bennett alone. "You told me that all my husband had was a cold. You're a liar. If you had diagnosed him correctly, I could have gotten him some help!"

"Brya, listen to me. The early signs of this disease resemble . . ."

"Resemble a cold, doctor? I've trusted you with our family through several crises so how could you be so stupid on this one?" Her tears were ready to spill over at any moment.

Doctor Bennett was speechless and couldn't argue against her. He waited a few moments and took a deep breath. "Your husband has a serious disease that affects the lungs and his breathing. He needs intense bed rest, mild exercise, and fresh air. If Holden doesn't get these things, he'll die. Most people who have this disease are sent to sanitariums."

When Brya heard the word sanitarium, she couldn't contain herself. "Nobody else in my family's going to a sanitarium! My mother died in one. Don't take my husband away from me, too."

Dr. Bennett held her shivering body while she sobbed. He had no idea about her background, and now was not the time to talk about it.

"Brya, this disease, for which there is no medicine, is very contagious. I have no idea where your husband picked it up, but you and Olivia stand a good chance of contracting tuberculosis if he stays on the farm."

"My husband stays! I won't let him leave. I can get him well."

"You are putting yourselves at grave risk. Please rethink your idea."

"You're wasting your breath, doctor. I've already made up my mind and no one is about to change it. My husband's staying at home with his family, where he belongs."

❧

The wicked, hot summer of 1934 lasted late into the fall. The dusty air never moved. No matter what Brya did, Holden got worse. His parents visited every chance they could until Maud, his mother, decided to stay with them on the farm. Brya couldn't blame her.

Megan telephoned numerous times, wanting to help, but Brya refused. The disease was too contagious and it just wasn't safe.

They tried every home remedy imaginable—from mustard plasters to putting burning candles on his chest with glasses over them to extract the poison out of his lungs. Cod liver oil was used to flush his bowels, but nothing seemed to help. Holden continued to waste away in the bed.

Olivia was brought in periodically to see her daddy. Not too close, just so she could see him. This made her smile. She could now say "Da-da." When Holden was somewhat coherent, he'd manage a tiny smile in response to his daughter's words.

Maud and Brya had to tend to the farm themselves. Maud took care of the house, the baby, and kept an eye on her son. Brya had to hand it to her; she was made of sturdy stock and knew how to be helpful without upsetting the apple cart. Brya knew it was ripping her heart out to watch Holden like this, but so far she hadn't shed a tear. Maud truly believed he'd be fine again, and that kept Brya's spirits up.

Brya had the difficult chore of working the farm. She loathed stepping in the smelly chicken manure and cleaning the noisy hen house. All she used to do was collect the eggs, and that had been enough for her. Besides, she sneezed every time she stayed around the alfalfa too long. The work was overwhelming. Maud continued to make the meals, and they both tried to get some food into Holden's stomach.

Even though Holden's mother was tending to the inside of the house, it was beginning to be a shambles. It needed repainting and some repairs that neither of them knew how to do. Holden had tried to teach Brya how to paint, but to no avail. The smell of it nauseated her.

Olivia, fortunately, was old enough to sit up and play in her playpen. They could leave her in there to spend time with her toys, drink a bottle, and have a nap.

Brya looked forward to the evenings when the sun was setting. She could see Boggy Creek in the distance with the expanse of green fields in between. Then she could relax on the shaded porch. Maud stayed inside, to listen to the radio and crochet.

Brya placed her head against the back of the rocking chair, gazed out at the yellow and pink Oklahoma sky, rocked Olivia, and thought about her dying love. Wasn't there anything she could do to stop this savage disease from invading his body? Sometimes, when she sat alone, she heard him moan in pain and cough endlessly. It might be better for him to pass than to suffer on, but that would be the end of the world for her. No wonder her Mama Beatrice suffered so when she lost her husband.

As each day passed, the farm was becoming more and more of a burden. It was turning cold and Brya couldn't work the long hours that her husband did in the barnyard. Traveling to Boggy Creek was a chore now, even with Maud watching the baby. Consequently, food and minerals for the chickens were not being purchased as often as they should be. Several died.

Brya was getting nervous. When she would collect the eggs at dawn, she'd accidentally drop some and all she could think of was the money she lost. Their income started to sink right along with her husband's failing health. For the first time, she was really afraid. Holden was getting ready to leave her just like her daddy did. Her dreams of a family were fading fast. The bills were flowing in, and there was no money to pay them. Each day she grew more overwhelmed and lonely. Her saving grace was her daughter's smiling face. Where would she be without her?

By early November, all hope of keeping Holden alive was gone. Brya, with the help of her neighbors, moved his bed so that it faced the window. In a last ditch effort to create a moment of happiness for her husband and daughter, she ran out in the new, fluffy snow and made angel's wings. This fascinated the baby. She would lift her plump arms up in the air and try to do the same thing. This brought tears to Holden's eyes. Gone forever were the big plans they had made together.

By Thanksgiving, Holden had wasted away to nothing, and the farm was nearly in foreclosure. Brya cleaned up the congealed blood that her husband would cough up from his lungs; it smelled like the warm blood that poured out of her daddy. The doctor had insisted that she wear a face mask and gloves, and cover her hair. The baby couldn't be in her daddy's room anymore because he was too ill. Brya, afraid that Olivia might get sick too, would allow Corabelle and some of the women from church to keep Olivia overnight at their homes. It was difficult to have her away but Brya knew it was right.

One starry evening, as Brya lay beside her husband, she took his withered hand and held it close to her heart. His breaths were coming shorter and shorter now. Brya knew the end was near and couldn't bring herself to leave his side. The room smelled like death, musty and dank. Why couldn't she have helped him out of this? Why couldn't she have helped her daddy and her Mama Beatrice?

Suddenly, Holden opened his eyes and whispered to his wife to come close. She leaned in next to his face in order to hear. "I didn't mean to bring you this pain. And I never meant to leave you alone with a child to raise."

He stopped to catch his breath, his face twisted in pain.

"Promise me that you and Olivia will plant at least one rattlesnake watermelon seed and watch it grow."

Without warning he began to gurgle.

"You mean more to me than . . ."

"Holden, Holden!" Brya raised herself up off of his sunken chest and stared into his fixed, brown eyes. He didn't see her. She ran her hands through his thick, black hair, and held his head to her breast. He was gone. Brya heard a wailing sound and didn't realize it was coming from her until Maud came running through the door. She fell on the edge of the bed and wept, too. After a while, Brya stood up and helped Maud to her feet.

Then she reached down, closed Holden's eyes and pulled the sheet over his face.

Brya walked into Olivia's room and stared at her sleeping baby. "Oh, my God, your daddy's dead, Olivia. Your daddy's dead." The child continued to sleep peacefully. She walked into the living room and clung to Maud, and they cried together. Later, Brya went back into Olivia's bedroom and lifted her up to her breast. She needed to feel her warm body next to her but the memory of losing her family once before still loomed like a dark terror in the middle of the night. She carried the baby to her husband's room and covered her with a quilt. Brya curled up on the floor with her and wondered if the night would be kind, or if the memory of Holden would haunt her dreams like everyone else had. She pulled Olivia close, afraid to fall asleep. Maud walked in, stared at her son, then silently returned to her bedroom to grieve alone.

Early the next morning, Brya telephoned the mortuary to come take Holden away. Next, she called Grandpa Patch and Grandma Eugenia. Maud wanted them to go down and tell Virgil so that he wouldn't be alone when he heard the news.

Holden was supposed to be carrying in the turkey and helping with holiday festivities. Instead, his body was being taken back to Cimarron to be buried there.

Patch, older and more bent over now, came to fetch Brya once again, this time in Boggy Creek. Virgil had also made the drive to bring home his grief-stricken wife. It was calming for Brya to ride alongside her grandpa again. This time, there were no horrors to see along the side of the road. Had there been any, she would've fallen apart. Olivia was too young to know or understand what had happened, so she sat up in the back seat, quietly playing with her favorite toy. The ride on the bumpy road lulled her to sleep.

At twenty-one, Brya was facing a fifth death in her family. First her parents, then her baby boys, and now the love of her life. When they arrived in Cimarron, Eugenia, dressed in black, was there to greet her. This time, all they shared were tears.

Brya requested that the funeral be outside, even though it was a cold day. Holden would have liked it that way. Family and friends arrived with outstretched arms. But Holden's brother Mark sat alone and wept. Megan came with her fiancé, James. Corabelle and Bud left their farming duties to assist in any way they could. Even the neighborhood collie, Jamie, sat poised at the gravesite. Holden had wrapped his torn leg after he was hit by a car. The dog never forgot.

Letters, expressing sympathetic words, came mostly from people that Brya didn't know. But they had known Holden since he was a little boy.

Brya stood alone, gripping her daughter. She had no more tears to shed, having cried and cried for days. She didn't listen to one word that Rev. Riley said. Instead, she heard the rustle of the chestnut trees, and a new voice from inside her emerged. She was through with emotion, and finished with getting hurt. Her life would change after this because there would never be another love like Holden Hunter. She was pretty enough to get a rich man, and capable enough to raise her daughter. She fully intended to leave the hard life behind.

Rev. Riley interrupted her thoughts and reminded her that "it was time."

With complete composure, she took Olivia over to her daddy's gravesite, removed her gloves, and pulled a small seed out of her black coat. Grandpa Patch handed her a spade, and she proceeded to move just enough earth to plant the watermelon seed at the head of his coffin. She slowly covered the seed up with some loose soil, kissed her fingers, and placed them on top.

"Good-bye, my dear, sweet Holden," she whispered. "I'll never love another like I have you."

Olivia copied her mother and kissed her fingers, too, placing them on top of the nearby ground. At Brya's prompting, her little nine-month-old stood there waving good-bye to her daddy as they lowered his coffin into the ground.

Afterwards, the families gathered at the Hunter home. Maud and Virgil were in shock, and Brya did everything she could to console them. Olivia did the best job of all by just being her sweet self.

Several days after the funeral, Bud and Corabelle came to get Brya and drove her back to the farm to take care of the business of letting it go, while Olivia stayed with her great-grandparents. The bank was in the process of repossessing the farm which left Brya with very little money. As soon as everything was liquidated, she'd go back to Cimarron to talk to Patch about what to do next. He was the only one that could help.

The farm looked desolate. Brya had a few things to gather up, and then planned to leave Muddy Boggy Creek for good.

It was difficult to set foot in their bedroom again. Too many memories. She glanced around the silent, dirty room. The mortuary staff had taken the mattress and bed clothes that Holden used and burned them. There was only her mama's daybed. She could never let that go. She asked Corabelle and Bud to load up Holden's truck with her few belongings. She was only keeping one picture of Holden, for Olivia, but didn't think that she would be able to look at it for a long time. Once again, her guardian angel that

Eusabia promised was nowhere to be found despite the repeated pats on her shoulder.

As Brya gathered up her clothes, she came across her dusty jar with the forgotten five hundred dollars. She'd ask her grandpa if she needed to use it to pay off her debts.

With the help of her neighbors, Brya was packed in a couple of hours. The bank was taking all the rest. Bud and Corabelle said they'd keep her overnight on their farm and then they'd help drive the pickup to Cimarron the next day. That was fine because she didn't want to spend a night alone there. As Brya was about to leave, she noticed that she had left the paperweight she'd given Holden as a wedding gift on the window sill. It held the Fitzgibbon's soil in it. She picked it up, walked out the front door, and smashed it against the front steps, with the rest of her lost dreams.

Critical Decisions

Brya found it hard to have to go back and live with her grandparents but she needed their help. She was coming to them with her hat in her hand, and she did not know where to go, or what to do next.

South Drury Lane hadn't changed much in the few years she'd been gone. If anything, it was more beautiful. Grand oak trees and rich remains of lush vegetation painted a far prettier picture than the desolate dust bowl of Oklahoma.

"Hello, Grandpa," Brya shouted.

He came out of the kitchen to greet her, with Olivia hanging off of his hand.

"Hello, Brya. We're sure glad to see that pretty face of yours. Besides, I'm just getting too old to have to be so young with this daughter of yours."

Olivia was grinning from ear to ear, eager for a hug from her mama. Brya took off her wool coat, picked up her baby, and sat down in the living room. As she held Olivia close to her, she felt empty.

"Grandpa, I'm so lost. The bank took the farm. I couldn't take care of it like Holden did."

Patch sat down beside her, placing his hand on her leg. "The bank in Boggy Creek called me, Brya, bankers are a pretty close fraternity, you know. You had no control over what happened, and not one soul blames you."

Brya broke down into tears. "Grandpa, may Olivia and I stay here with you until I figure out what to do next?"

"Certainly, you can stay. Your grandma will be thrilled to have some female company." He hugged her close. "Everything will be all right, sweetheart."

❦

On the heels of Thanksgiving, the mood was sad and quiet. Brya felt lost and left behind, consumed with feelings that alternated between depression and anxiety. Making plans for the rest of her life was crucial and she didn't have a clue where to start. She had never really looked any further than staying on the farm and raising rattlesnake watermelons. A new husband was out of the question.

Olivia seemed to have trouble dealing with the change. She was grumpy and out of sorts, probably because the fluffy yellow chickens and the ornery rooster weren't around to entertain her anymore. She crawled into her great-grandpa's lap repeatedly, where she appeared to feel safe.

One evening after dinner, Eugenia spoke. Excitement danced in her eyes. "You're such a pretty young girl, why don't you see if you can get a job selling clothes in a women's dress shop, in a nice store, or something like that? The change would do you good, Brya."

Brya looked at her grandma questioningly.

Patch interrupted. "Why don't you journey down to the drugstore first thing in the morning and buy the *Oklahoma City Gazette*, a big-city newspaper. It has classified ads that might give you some ideas about what opportunities are available."

Brya's spirits began to pick up. "Maybe I could go out west and find a job by Megan. Then Olivia and I could be near her."

Grandma nodded in agreement as they discussed all the possibilities.

"All right, I'll go to the drugstore tomorrow." Brya squeezed her grandparents' hands, then excused herself to find her daughter's favorite blanket.

Olivia was unusually receptive for bed and easy to tuck in. When Brya got undressed for bed, she felt a sudden chill down her spine. The winter wind howled outside as she tossed her nightgown quickly over her head. She made sure the window was tightly closed then cocooned herself inside the covers.

As she drifted off to sleep, she found herself dancing under the stars with Holden once again. And then her daddy cut in. Her wedding dress swirled in the moonlight as he held her close. Suddenly, the music stopped. Brya was alone, brushing gray and jellied insides off her dress.

Terrified, she sat up in bed, her heart pounding out of her chest. She couldn't scream for fear of waking up the household, but she couldn't sleep after that, either. She lay in bed shivering until morning.

At a shockingly early hour, Brya got out of bed, threw some warm clothes on, and walked to town. When she passed one of the side streets, she saw Holden's parents' house. It was strange not to see her husband outside working or walking down the street to be with her. Virgil had had a stroke right after Holden's funeral. Another son's death was just too much for him.

It was a lonely walk to the drugstore, with Holden in every memory. He had always walked with her, held her hand, and stopped to kiss her. Brya so wanted to feel close to him again, watch him kick the autumn leaves from beneath his feet, and tell his silly jokes. She looked for him in everything, from the old schoolhouse to the hideaway where they used to get lost in each other's bodies. A tear rolled down her cheek. She had so many unanswered questions. Why did it have to end like it did? Why were all her dreams shattered? It was so difficult to move on.

By the time she reached Green's Drugstore, she was overcome with sadness. Mr. Green was energetically sweeping the entrance with an old broom.

"Howdy, Brya. I was so sorry to hear about your husband, him being so young and all."

"Thank you, Mr. Green. We all miss him more than you'll ever know." Brya couldn't say anymore. She grabbed the newspaper, threw the change on the counter next to the Bazooka bubble gum, and shot past the shopkeeper. She didn't like him anyway. He always looked her up and down, licking his lips.

She ran most of the way back to her grandparents' house, headed straight to the dining room table, and spread the newspaper wide open to the classified ad section. Her grandma was having a cup of hot cocoa and feeding Olivia her breakfast. "Do you want some hot cocoa, dear?" she asked.

"Yes, ma'am. I haven't had any breakfast, and it was very chilly outside this morning."

Brya poured over the long list of want ads, amazed at what was offered. Most of the jobs for women were for store clerks, schoolteachers, or nurses. Brya swirled the cocoa around in her mouth, savoring the flavor before she swallowed. She looked under "Out of State." A few drops splattered on the newspaper, and she brushed it off with her sweater sleeve as Grandma Eugenia sat nearby, looking on. Grandma spotted an ad for a cosmetologist in a fine cosmetics store in Santa Fe, New Mexico. She explained to Brya that it was a beautiful part of the country where rich people travel on vacations.

Brya looked into her grandma's eyes. "What're you trying to say?"

"You and Olivia need to start over, and you also need to get away from your memories here. I can see how sad you are every time you walk down the street." She touched her granddaughter's face. "You have incredible skin, and a great figure. I bet you could easily sell expensive cosmetics, because women will want your beautiful skin."

Brya blushed.

"You're young, and with your personality you could make a nice living and meet some fascinating people. Brya, you could have the world by the tail."

It surprised Brya that her grandma thought of all these things. "But I don't have any experience with cosmetics. Why, I don't even wear much makeup." She ran her hand across her face.

She showed Brya the ad again. "The 'Nina Nicholson Company' is willing to train you, plus pay your way to the interview if you qualify."

"Okay, Grandma, I'll think about it. It sounds like fun playing with all that makeup and putting it on other people, like playing dress-up." Brya recalled Mama Beatrice's vanity where she and her sisters used to spend hours putting on cosmetics, trying to look like big girls. Her mama kept large jars of cold cream around for just those occasions. After the girls were through making a mess of Mama Beatrice's dressing table, she would patiently help them remove the colors from their faces, and the furniture, too.

"Grandma, let's talk to Grandpa this evening and see what he thinks. I'm beginning to like the idea." Brya put the newspaper on the end table next to the sofa in the living room, and let out a sigh. If Patch agreed to this job interview, then maybe this would be the answer to a new existence.

When her grandpa came home that night he looked weary. Brya wasn't sure whether or not to approach him about the job, but tired or not, he was usually willing to talk.

"Grandpa," she said peering into the living room where he was sitting. "May I speak with you about an ad in the newspaper that I found today?"

"Go ahead," he said, pushing his glasses to the end of his nose. He was propped up in his favorite easy chair. For the first time, Brya noticed that his hair was white as snow.

"Grandpa," Brya burst forth. "There's an advertisement for a cosmetologist in Santa Fe, New Mexico. The store caters to the wealthy, and they'll train me for the job." She stopped to listen to his response.

He got up, took her hand and walked her over to the couch. After he had studied her face for a moment, he said, "Brya, I'm an old man who has led many lives. I'd be a fool to stop you from jumping at a chance to make a new one. You've had nothing but one heartache after another. It would probably be a good move towards making a new start." He laughed and added, "I could insist that you stay here and let me turn you into a banker, but that wouldn't suit your personality. Use your talents well, and life will give back what you put into it."

Patch glanced at the ad that Brya had circled. "I think that it would be best to call the Nina Nicholson Company first thing in the morning, and tell them that you're interested. Be sure to inquire about the salary and their plans for the future."

Brya was delighted with her grandpa's response. The rest of the evening was spent sitting around the fireplace, playing with Olivia on the floor. They cringed as the sleet hit the windows. It was a perfect night for a murder mystery on the radio. Instead, Brya and her grandpa listened to a big band leader named Duke Ellington. Not her cup of tea.

Brya awoke to a gloomy, winter day. The wind was still howling and the gray sky looked ominous. She hoped this wasn't a bad omen. At first, when she tried to call Santa Fe, she had trouble with the phone lines. But after an hour, it cleared up and she got through.

Her armpits were perspiring as she heard the phone ringing at the company, and then, "Good morning, Nina Nicholson Company. May I help you?"

Her grandpa always said that a cowgirl has to dance, so she better get dancing. "Um, good morning," she said. "I've called about your advertisement for a cosmetologist."

She was passed through to Fran Shepard, Miss Nicholson's personal assistant. It seemed like an eternity before the woman picked up the phone. Just when Brya forgot she was waiting, a strange voice said, "Mrs. Shepard."

Patch had also told her to have confidence in herself and not act shy on the telephone, and be sure to have good manners.

"Good morning, Mrs. Shepard," Brya answered, summoning up all her courage. "My name is Brya Hunter and I'm calling you from Cimarron, Oklahoma, about your advertisement for a cosmetologist."

In a pleasant voice, the woman replied, "I'm in charge of finding that one special woman to fill this job opening. This is why we're advertising all over the country. Experience, oddly enough, is not necessary. Nina Nicholson would rather train the new person, provided she's the right one. We're scouting for a special look and if you fit that criteria, then the company will bring you here for an interview."

"What type of look do you want?" Brya asked.

"A trim, young, blonde woman," she said, "one with a fresh face that can be made up to look like we want her to look."

Without thinking, the words flew out of her mouth. "Mrs. Shepard, I believe I'm the one!" Brya winced. She had said too much. But the woman liked her forthrightness.

Brya added, "I wear a size 6, and I have long blonde hair, blue-green eyes, and hardly ever apply makeup.

People tell me that I don't need it. But I love makeup, and that's why I'm calling." Brya made a quick recovery on that one, and hoped it worked.

"Are you single, Brya?"

"Yes, I am. My husband has just passed away, and I'm trying to find a new life for myself."

"I'm sorry about your husband. I lost mine, as well, two years ago."

It was nice to know that Mrs. Shepard understood the way she felt.

"Let me add something else, dear," Mrs. Shepard said. "We like single women at Nina Nicholson's. Santa Fe is a small, elite community of very wealthy people that must be catered to."

Mrs. Shepard felt that Brya was an interesting prospect for Nina Nicholson, and she was willing to bring her out by train for the interview, provided a photo was sent ahead. She wanted Brya to think about what they had discussed, and she would call her back once Nina had seen the photo.

The pay was not as high as Brya would like, but most of the work would be on a commission basis, according to how much she sold. If she had an appealing look and was good with people, she should have no trouble making a good amount of money.

"I'm very interested in this job, Mrs. Shepard. I'll get a picture off to you as soon as possible."

"Don't wait too long because we've received calls from all over the country in response to this ad. I would hate for you to miss out on an opportunity to work with such a dynamic woman as Nina."

"I won't take long, I promise. Thank you, Mrs. Shepard." They hung up. Excitement shot through Brya like a lightning bolt and she started jumping up and down. She ran downstairs to tell her grandma, and then immediately called Patch at the bank. They were delighted.

From the living room, Brya heard Olivia sneeze. She
hoped she was not coming down with a cold. As she walked
towards the kitchen, she heard Eugenia talking to her grand-
child as she cut up a fresh apple for her. Brya's thoughts ran
wild. Oh, my God. What will I do with Olivia? If I must
appear single for this job, then how can I have a baby? And
I won't be able to support the two of us at first. Once again,
Brya needed to talk to her grandparents about what to do.
But she knew for a fact that they were too old to take care
of an active little one.

Later that evening, Brya confessed her concern for her
daughter to Patch. "I know it'll be a struggle for me at first,
but I'm torn between the world of motherhood and the need
to make a living. Eventually, I'll be able to provide a nice
home for us, but now I have to take care of business, even
at the risk of leaving my daughter with someone else for a
while."

"Perhaps Megan might be willing to keep Olivia in
California with her new husband, James, while you get
settled into your new job," Patch replied.

What a great idea, Brya thought. Olivia would have the
time of her life on the Cooper's new farm, and on top of
that, they were near the ocean. Who wouldn't love being on
a farm, close to the seashore? Patch believed this could be
the solution, at least until Brya was situated enough to bring
her daughter to her new home.

As Brya listened to what Patch suggested, she remembered the times she had felt like a terrible parent. Number
one, she had forgotten to change Olivia's soiled diapers
several times, because Holden was so ill. She cried for
hours out of discomfort. And, she never thought she had
enough time to play with her. But this was an even bigger
predicament.

"Grandpa, if I send Olivia to my sister, will that make me a bad person?" Brya gazed at him as tears began to well up in her eyes.

"No, sweetheart. Leaving her with a family member for a while won't make you a bad person. Sometimes we're faced with extraordinary situations that force us to make hard choices. You're not abandoning your child. You're only trying to provide her with a caring home until you are able to take care of yourself again."

Brya looked into her daughter's innocent face. The little one had come into the room to inspect a piece of string that was stuck inside the carpet. This child of hers was so inquisitive that she wouldn't sit still for a minute.

"Grandpa, do you think this could make Olivia hate me later?" Brya watched her child pick up the string and study it.

"I don't think so, Brya. When she's old enough to have all this explained to her, she'll understand you did what you had to do."

"I hope so."

Brya gathered Olivia up in her arms, wiped some food off her cheek, and playfully tugged on the string. She gave her a longer embrace than usual.

"I wish that your grandmother and I could keep Olivia with us, but we're getting on in years," Patch said. "I'm worried we might not be able to keep such an active youngster in our home."

Eugenia nodded her head though tears filled her eyes as she looked over at mother and child.

When Patch heard the clock on the mantle strike nine, he rose up from his easy chair and hugged all his family goodnight. It was becoming harder and harder for him to climb the stairs, but somehow he always made the journey. He had been the Rock of Gibraltar for Brya. Now she wondered what she would do without him.

Brya slept close to her baby that night, tormented by the fear of leaving her. Her dreams plagued her, too. Lost and bewildered, she walked on the parched earth alongside the migrants, her stomach churning at the smell of sweat, dust, and decay. Her ear caught the loud cry of a desperate child begging for food. The destitute little one, hollowed from hunger, was Olivia. Paralyzed, Brya awoke, unable to catch her breath. She gasped, forcing the air into her lungs. My God, what is happening to me? Tomorrow, she'd speak with Eugenia about the nightmare. But the conversation never took place. Instead, she was preoccupied with getting ready to have her picture taken and sent off to the Nina Nicholson Company.

It didn't take Mrs. Shepard long to call once she received Brya's impressive photo. "Due to the approaching holidays, we are not scheduling interviews until the first of next year. We will take care of your travel arrangements, however, and send you an itinerary and interview schedule. In the meantime, enjoy your holidays and please know that Miss Nina is looking forward to meeting you."

Brya hung the phone up in a hurry and shouted, "Grandma, Grandpa, I got the interview!"

Another gloomy winter's day. It was difficult enough to call Megan, let alone look out of the window with no sun shining in. She'd wasted a week. Now she must do it. Brya called up the operator and gave her Megan's telephone number, STATION 5-8217.

"Hi Megan, it's Brya, how are you doing?"

"I'm so happy I think I've gone to heaven. How are you?"

She swallowed. "We're just fine, I guess, but I have a very large favor to ask of you. I can't stay here in Oklahoma—too many things remind me of Holden. I'm interviewing for a job in Santa Fe, New Mexico. I really want to be nearer to you, but that is the closest that I can get."

"What kind of job, Brya?"

"It's as a cosmetologist for one of Nina Nicholson's salons."

Megan is delighted. Nina Nicholson was known everywhere. "It will be just great for Olivia and you to leave and start over."

Brya took another deep breath. "About that special request, sis. The company wants me to appear unmarried so that I can mingle with the clientele better. Also, I'll be working mostly on commission, so I don't think I can make enough money to support us at first."

Megan immediately understood. "You want us to care for your child, don't you? Oh honey, I'd love to have her here. I'm sure James won't mind, but let me check with him just to be sure. He'll love her just like she's his very own."

"Thanks, sis. I'll owe you a big favor one day."

Megan suggested that if Brya got the job, she and James meet Brya and Olivia in Santa Fe. They could pick up Olivia there so that Brya could get settled. Besides, they would enjoy a little vacation after the holidays.

"Oh Megan, you've always been there for me. I don't know what I would do without you. I'll let you know how the interview goes and then we can make our plans. Give my love to James, and Megan, thanks a million."

Brya grinned from ear to ear as she put down the phone. She will be starting a new life, leaving the past behind. Her child will be safe, and she'll be working in a beautiful, wealthy town in New Mexico. What more could she ask?

The sun was finally trying to peek through the clouds. Maybe this was a good sign.

Brya realized that she had one more hurdle to jump. Would her grandparents continue taking care of Olivia until after her interview? She'd find out at dinner.

Their meal together was a joyous occasion. The grandparents said it wouldn't be any trouble to take care of the little one for a short while.

❧

Christmas was ghastly for Brya. Holden wouldn't be around to put the star on the top of the tree, carve the roast beef, or sneak a lick of icing from Eugenia's cake bowl. How would she manage to get through it? Brya wished she could be on her way to Santa Fe and avoid celebrating altogether.

But for Olivia, Christmas was a magical time. There were twinkling tree lights to grab (and be told not to), and brightly wrapped presents to try and unwrap before their time. She loved to play with the shiny, silver tinsel. She'd pick it off the tree and dangle it in front of her, then shake it off her hand. Christmas was all about this little girl, and the whole family rallied. She called Grandpa "Thanta Caus" because of his thick, white shock of hair. Grandpa Patch would swoop her up in his arms, and take her to the window to look for Santa's reindeers. Then he'd point to the ceiling and have her listen for their hoofbeats on the roof. Her eyes danced with excitement, trying to listen. She helped divert the family's attention away from the sadness in their hearts. The Hunters came over often during this time to enjoy their granddaughter, but they usually didn't stay for long. Maud would eventually start to cry and have to leave. Virgil needed help getting to the car, so Patch would drive them.

When Christmas and New Year's were over, Brya was relieved. It was time to break away from all of the pain and depression.

❧

Brya ran from the mailbox waving her train ticket in the air. She almost tripped over herself racing up the front porch steps. "Grandma, the ticket is here! I'll be on my way soon."

Eugenia scurried through the kitchen doorway and arrived out of breath. Inside the envelope was a letter and a train ticket. Brya was to be in Santa Fe by January 9, and have her interview the next day. It was already January 2, so there was not much time to prepare.

"Grandma, what on earth am I going to wear for this interview? I have nothing suitable for Santa Fe."

"If I were you, Brya, I'd buy myself a nice dark suit. You need to look professional."

Brya had never worn a suit in her life, and lately, all she'd worn were loose fitting farm clothes.

"Will you help me pick it out?"

"We'll go today, if you want. We have been glued here all through the holidays. Besides, Olivia will love the trip to town."

Brya glanced down at her wristwatch to make sure that they had plenty of time.

Eugenia headed to her bedroom to get ready. "I'll meet you downstairs inside of an hour," she said, closing the bedroom door behind her.

It had been a long time since Brya had gone on a shopping trip with her grandma. In fact, the last time was right before she married Holden. Eugenia was good at spotting that perfect outfit, and besides, she was interesting to talk to and held nothing back.

The two women were eager to embark on their expedition, so it didn't take long to reach downtown. Olivia snuggled in her pram, and covered with two warm blankets, seemed as excited as Brya and Eugenia. She loved to watch her breath linger in the air. This entertained her on the way to the store.

About a year ago, a middle-aged woman by the name of Vivien Rogers had opened up a new dress shop, and Brya and Eugenia heard it was doing well. She was originally from Tulsa, and stocked clothes that were a little more sophisticated than what Cimarron had to offer.

As the women entered the store, a fragrant scent filled the air. All the clothes were artistically displayed and easy to see. A nicely dressed woman, with her hair back in a bun, greeted them. She was wearing a brown wool dress that suited her shape, and low-heeled, matching leather shoes. "Hello, I'm Vivien Rogers. May I help you?"

This woman was someone from whom Brya could learn to sell. The way she met them was so appealing and sincere. Brya continued to observe her.

"Vivien, my granddaughter is leaving soon for an interview with the Nina Nicholson Company in Santa Fe. She needs a nice suit for the interview, and we wonder if you carry such a thing?"

"I most definitely have several lovely suits to choose from." She bent down, offering a small stuffed rabbit to Olivia. "Come with me."

Miss Rogers held up a forest green suit that she thought would look good with Brya's complexion. She wasn't wrong. When Brya came out of the dressing room, they raved about how sophisticated she looked. Brya held her long hair up in order to look at herself in the full-length mirror.

"Mrs. Hunter, I think you should wear your hair up for the interview. What little I know about Nina Nicholson is that all her saleswomen have to appear spectacular. That means taking good care of oneself. And you especially need to keep up with the changing styles."

Brya appreciated her expert advice, and thought about everything she told her.

Eugenia generously offered to buy Brya the suit, plus another dress as a gift. The outfits would be modeled for Patch that evening, just to get a man's reaction.

❦

"The suit's a little skimpy, the way it shows off your figure and all," Patch said.

Eugenia winked at Brya. "You can't keep her a baby forever, Patch, and besides, this is the style."

He mumbled to himself, then changed the subject. Something else was on his mind. "Stop modeling and sit down by me," he said.

"The other day, Brya, you mentioned the five hundred dollars that had been tucked away. You wondered when you should spend it."

"Yes, Grandpa."

"Well, I've been doing some thinking. And just as I said before, as long as I'm able, I'll help you out financially, so don't spend your five hundred dollars yet. I'll send you on the train with enough money for food, and for a down payment on an apartment in Santa Fe, should you get the job. Rent one before you come back to collect Olivia and your belongings. The five hundred dollars can help you through after you start working. However, I think you should consider giving some of the money to Megan for taking care of Olivia."

That sounded more than fair to her. After all, he and Eugenia had taken them in, and made sure they were comfortable. Now, it was time for Brya to try and make it on her own.

❦

It was freezing cold, and the smoke from the train stack swirled through the air. Eugenia made a full meal at home to tide Brya over on the journey. The grandparents wouldn't have to wait long because it was time for Brya to board the train.

"Wish me luck," she said as she planted a steady foot on the train steps.

"We send our prayers with you," Eugenia replied.

Brya was eager to get on the train and warm herself up.

"Call if you need anything," Patch yelled.

"I will, Grandpa." As Brya blew a kiss to Olivia and the train door closed behind her, she looked back and saw her daughter's tiny hand wave "Bye-bye." In the middle of all the excitement, her heart wanted to break.

❦

Traveling west was a unique experience, and the dawn brought new scenery. Brya was still tired after a restless night of dozing.

An old Negro conductor with a limp had taken her ticket as she boarded the train. Now he woke her up. "Would you like some juice, young lady?"

"Well, that's mighty nice of you. I'd appreciate something to drink, my mouth's a little dry." She rubbed her tongue along the top of her teeth and grimaced from the bad taste. Luckily, her toothbrush was in reach. After breakfast, she'd head to the bathroom and freshen up.

The conductor started to walk away. "I'll be right back with your drink."

"By the way," Brya said, "where are we? This is my first train trip."

"Why, I can't believe it's your first trip. We're almost to the Oklahoma state line." Brya glanced out of the window. "This is where most of the farmers are losing their crops. It's the 'long arm of Oklahoma,' better known as the Panhandle. I'll show you a map, and you'll see what I mean." As Brya's hand traced the outline of the state she could see the resemblance between a pan's handle and the shape of the state.

The conductor left to get her juice, and she resumed staring out the dusty window. The Oklahoma Panhandle was desolate. It had become a graveyard of farms, and a graveyard for humans as well. Brya would be glad to get through this area, just like she was when she came face to face with the migrants. A large, ebony hand tapped her on the shoulder and handed her a chilled glass of cold juice. "This hits the spot. By the way, what's your name?" asked Brya.

"Monroe, Monroe Adams," he proudly replied. "It's mighty nice of you to ask my name. Not many white folks care about what a Negra's name is."

"When I was a little girl, Monroe, I knew a wonderful Negro woman and her name was Eusabia. She used to cook for my family, and we loved her very much. She taught me about guardian angels, and told me that if I pat my shoulder, a guardian angel will always come and take care of me."

"Whatever happened to this Eusabia?"

"I don't know, Monroe, I just don't know. But she'll always be in my heart."

The scenery changed once the train got closer to Santa Fe. Deep, rugged canyons and table-topped mesas covered in snow dotted the skyline. Varying shades of red and pink rock lay like puzzle pieces everywhere. Mountains looked like ant hills under an ever-changing sky. Every view was a picture postcard. Brya wondered if Santa Fe was surrounded by all this beauty, or had the Depression ruined it, too? Supposedly, rich people and artists lived there. She wondered where they came from, and how they survived the Depression.

The train pulled in about 1:30 in the afternoon. Monroe said that the town was within walking distance to the plaza. As Brya stretched up from her seat and glanced out the window, the buildings were completely different looking, like ones she had only seen in *Life* magazine. As she stepped off the train, and put her feet on solid ground, she felt as though the train was still moving underneath her. She stood there for a moment, trying to get her balance and take it all in. The air was crisp and chilly. Brya pulled her wool coat around her noticing the Spanish architecture. From where she stood, only squared-off adobe houses could be seen connected together like apartments.

She stopped a tall, rugged cowboy with a broad grin, and asked how to get to town. He gladly gave her directions. Monroe was right. The train station was only a couple of blocks away from the plaza square.

It felt great to be able to walk after such a long trip. Brya noticed something else, too. Here in this new and different place she felt free. The pain and horrors of the past year belonged to another place and time.

Shortly, she came upon the La Fonda Hotel with the Chapel of Loretta next door. Before going inside, she stood in the entrance with her hands cupped over her eyes, and gazed out over the plaza. When she entered the hotel lobby, she was greeted by a warm, mesquite-wood fire in the massive fireplace. A chandelier of antlers hung in the center of the room and the worn leather chairs looked inviting.

"Where is the Nina Nicholson salon?" she asked the desk clerk.

"Just a few doors down the street," he replied. "We have several brochures about the area that you may have."

After she checked in, she headed upstairs to rest. Her body was tired from the long train ride. The room was cozy, with over-stuffed furniture and a big bed. She laid her heavy suitcase down, flopped on the bed, and immediately fell asleep.

After her nap, she decided to visit where her interview was going to take place. Downtown Santa Fe was unique. The buildings were constructed of authentic adobe and pinion pine.

The Nina Nicholson Company, located next to the First National Bank of Santa Fe, had two doors that resembled giant slabs of Indian turquoise trimmed with gold. Two scrolled capital "N's" graced the front of them. Brya liked the place just for the way it looked from the outside.

Since she didn't have to think about the interview till eight the next morning, she wandered toward the downtown plaza to get a feel for the area, and whether or not she'd like to live here. She picked up a lot of reading material along the way, and found out that the Palace of the Governors was not a palace but the oldest seat of government in the United States. Renovations were currently underway. Next, she decided to go into the Chapel of Loretta. It was best known for its circular staircase that had no center support—an engineering marvel. As she stood alone looking up at the stained glass, she felt at peace.

Her stomach reminded her that she hadn't eaten since early morning, so Brya went back to the hotel for a supper of the best cheese enchiladas she'd ever had. She thought about Grandpa Patch and the fact that many years ago he traveled on the Santa Fe Trail as a young wrangler. How could a place that was so old make her feel so new?

The next day, as Brya descended the winding steps to the lobby wearing her new green suit, a few heads turned. She blushed, trying to ignore several older men who stared over their newspapers at her. A couple of them took long drags off their cigarettes while they gawked. She adjusted her skirt, hoping that it was not too short, and continued walking. She'd taken Vivien's advice and pulled her hair back in a tortoise shell barrette held at the nape of her neck, even though this was not a look that she was used to. When she reached the Nina Nicholson salon, she took a deep breath, swallowed, and entered, exuding all the confidence that she could muster.

A fragrant smell of lilac filled the display room. She walked around slowly, enjoying the merchandise. There were different counters for different products, all displayed in regal gold and glass bottles or wrappers. The large double "N" was engraved on all of Nina's creations. There was not a salesperson in sight. As Brya checked her makeup in a mirror, she started to get a little nervous. Just before it got the best of her, she heard a soft, low voice coming from behind her. Startled, Brya turned and Nina Nicholson placed a manicured hand in her clammy one, and shook it, knowing full well who she was.

Nina, commanding and elegant, stood about six feet tall. The black dress she was wearing accentuated every curve she had, and confidence oozed from every pore. With her high cheek bones and chiseled features, she looked like a high-fashion model. Nina began their meeting by complimenting Brya on the color of her suit and how it accentuated her fine features. She was also impressed with her ability to look so 'put together' at a young age.

"Thank you, Miss Nicholson," Brya said, silently thanking Vivien.

"What do you think of my store?"

"I feel like I'm in a palace, Miss Nicholson. You sell so many gorgeous things here, and I especially like your front doors."

Nina smiled and offered Brya a seat and some hot tea. She watched her like a hawk as she sat down, then crossed her long legs and asked, "Have you ever sold anything before?"

"Well, ma'am, just our chickens that we had on our farm in Muddy Boggy Creek. My husband and I sold them for food. That's how we made our living."

Nina laughed out loud, then studied her for a minute. "It's probably a lot harder selling chickens than selling cosmetics."

She picked up a long black cigarette holder, put a cigarette in it, and lit up. "There is something that you ought to know. I have a wealthy clientele from every part of the country. Cater to them." Nina lightly flicked an ash in a nearby ashtray and continued. "Brya, I'm impressed that you look classy, but I'm wondering how such an extraordinary young woman can come out of Muddy Boggy Creek, Oklahoma? Do you think that you can work here in my company?"

"Oh, yes ma'am—anything's better than selling chickens. I used to love to make myself up when I was a little girl. My mama was a beautiful woman who used to let me put on her makeup, and dress up in her clothes and shoes."

"Where did you grow up, Brya?"

Her face changed instantly. "Well," she hesitated, "I lived in Trinity, Oklahoma until my parents died, and then I moved to Cimarron to be with my grandparents." She couldn't say anymore.

Nina noticed that this was a sensitive topic and immediately changed the subject. "Do you have a husband?"

"Holden, that was my husband, passed on from tuberculosis last year."

"I'm so sorry to hear that you've lost so many people in your young life. You must be looking forward to starting over."

"Oh, yes. You see, Miss Nicholson, I have a baby daughter. She's staying with my sister in California until I get situated. Later on, if I get this job, I want to bring her back with me to live."

Nina took a long, last drag on her cigarette, then laid it down in the ashtray. "I appreciate the assets of single women, and I'm impressed with your honesty about your daughter. It's good that you are planning ahead. What's her name?"

"Olivia."

"What a beautiful name. I'll have to invent a new fragrance after her."

Brya was touched.

"I've interviewed lots of young women in my day, Brya, and none of them have your potential, nor your obvious good upbringing," Nina said. "How does six hundred dollars a month, plus a 7% commission, sound to you?"

"That sounds fine. Great!" Brya stammered.

They talked until noon about all the details: when the job training would start, where Brya could live so she could walk to work, and so on. It appeared that Nina and Brya would have no problem working together. However, now it was up to Brya to find a place to live, get back to Cimarron, collect her daughter and her belongings, and arrive back in time for job training at the end of the month.

After a hurried lunch of chicken salad and a root beer float, Brya set out to look for a place to live. Nina had given her a list of names to contact, so it didn't take her long to secure a small one-bedroom apartment near the store. The landlord knew Nina well, and because of her, gave Brya a special deal. Brya didn't have to pay rent for the first month.

In one day, Brya acquired a new job and a new place to live. She raced back to the hotel to telephone her grandparents and make a train reservation back to Cimarron.

Flurries of snow drifted softly against the train window as Brya headed back to Cimarron. The red-tinged Sangre de Cristo Mountains slowly disappeared from view. Brya entertained herself with a book of Sherlock Holmes mysteries that she bought in Santa Fe. Challenged by whodunits, the two-day train trip went by quickly and once again, she was greeted by her family.

Olivia threw her arms around her mother's neck and babbled on about snow, and things no one could quite make out. Patch drilled Brya about Santa Fe and her new job as they made their way home.

When Brya reached the house, she telephoned Megan to tell her the good news. The two sisters set a date to meet in Santa Fe, so that Megan and James could take Olivia home with them. Patch and Eugenia decided to come along to help Brya get settled. This would give them more time with Olivia, too.

"While you're still at home, Brya, I want to teach you how to be a smart businesswoman," Patch declared. "Even though you're going to a safe place during these hard times, you still need to know how to manage your money. I never want you to suffer again."

"What do you mean, Grandpa?"

"In the 1920s, Santa Fe experienced the Depression much like us, Brya. The drought and all. But out of that, two new industries rose up, mining and oil. Some people were able to make a lot of money because they were not in any debt. Properties were bought up with cash and the lucky ones could do whatever they wanted."

For the next two weeks, Brya attended "Grandpa Patch's Business School." She was a quick study, and responded favorably to his coaching. He talked with her about saving a portion of her money each week, about always conducting herself in a business-like manner, about the importance of loyalty, honesty, and the meaning of integrity. Brya could tell these were the principles that made her grandfather so successful, and such a good person.

❧

Brya enjoyed having her family travel back to Santa Fe with her; it wasn't as hard to leave this way. As the train pulled out of Cimarron and traveled down the rickety, old tracks, Brya watched out the window until she could no longer see a town. Cimarron and Muddy Boggy Creek were now just dots on the map of her past.

The weather improved as they traveled westward. Patch and Eugenia marveled over the same beauty that captivated Brya when she last came this way. It was their first visit here and they, too, were impressed with the majestic mountains, mesas, and deep canyons.

When the train arrived in Santa Fe, Brya knew what to do. The few blocks to the hotel would be too much for the grandparents to walk with their luggage, so Brya flagged down a porter, and for a generous tip, he carried their belongings for them. Brya's daybed and the rest of her clothing would follow. The crisp air was good for Patch and Eugenia, and although they were slow walkers, they enjoyed eyeing the Spanish and Indian influences along the way. Patch checked everyone in at the La Fonda while Eugenia marveled at the furniture in the lobby. It was a busy check-in time, so while Patch waited he read some brochures about the area. There was a Santa Fe ticket office just north of the hotel that arranged sightseeing tours of nearby Indian pueblos. They could even ride in a fifteen-passenger touring car. After breakfast the following day, that was the first thing he planned on having them all do.

Once they got to their hotel room, Olivia was restless and eager to play, so Brya let her grandparents rest while she took her child on a small excursion through the town plaza. It was Sunday, and all the stores were closed. But, when Brya showed her the huge doors at Nina Nicholson's, her eyes widened. She held her up to the window, where Olivia left tiny handprints while trying to look inside. Olivia loved to peer in at all the amber-colored bottles full of liquid surprises. After visiting Nina's, Brya took her daughter for some ice cream at the drugstore, but it was a task to keep the pink strawberry from dripping all over the child's dress; the warm inside air was melting it faster than her small, busy lips could take it in.

Back at the hotel, Patch and Eugenia were seated by the fireplace in the lobby, refreshed and ready to see their granddaughter's new apartment. It wasn't a very long walk to her new place. With key in hand, Brya opened the front door and Olivia ran inside. "Mama, Mama."

"You said my name, baby." Brya hugged Olivia's small body. "You're so adorable."

Brya's heart fell to her stomach, knowing what was soon to come. She walked towards a window carrying Olivia. "Sweetheart, Mama has something to tell you." Brya swallowed and sat down on the floor, with Olivia, holding her tiny hand, as she looked deep into the child's big green eyes. "Honey, Mama's going to live here for a while, and you're going to stay on your Aunt Megan's farm in California." Olivia looked around the white, undecorated living room, and then back at her mama.

"This will be our new home, eventually, sweetheart. I showed you where my work is, and when I make enough money, I'll bring you back here to live. Besides, I could never leave you for long. You'll get to go to the beach, gather sea shells, and build great big sandcastles. You'll be having such a good time, you won't even miss me." Olivia was too young to understand, and it was a good thing.

Brya really didn't know how long it would be before she could have Olivia back with her.

The next day, Patch and Eugenia took Brya on a shopping spree for her apartment. They found new sheets and a blanket for the daybed, a small kitchen table with two chairs, some kitchen supplies, and a piece of Indian pottery. After Brya made some money, she would buy more furniture and clothing. Until then, she'd just have to wait. The apartment felt like a little doll house to her.

Megan and James arrived the following day. California had done Megan well; she even had a tan. It was nice to see James under better circumstances. His sun-streaked brown hair framed his dark eyes. He gave a hearty handshake, and was masculine and strong in every way. It was apparent that he loved Megan more than anything. Brya was happy for her sister.

After two days of sightseeing, eating too much Mexican food, and getting to know the area, it was time for everyone to leave.

Patch and Eugenia were the first to go. They had made sure that Brya was situated, and that their great-granddaughter would be taken care of, as well. Brya put her arms around her grandpa, and remembered that long drive out of Trinity with a man she didn't even know but had learned to love and honor. She prayed that this was not the last time she would see both of them alive. Eugenia placed a hand on Brya's shoulder, looked into her sad eyes and said, "I know how difficult this is for you." Brya hugged her, sobbing into her neck. Brya could smell her warm, musty smell that she'd grown to love. What would she do without both of them to guide her?

Patch, as usual, couldn't leave without giving a little more advice. "Take care of yourself and then nothing can go wrong. Don't let anyone talk you into anything that you don't want to do, and above all, don't let your emotion overshadow your reason." He said he loved her and to call them as much as she could. Patch and Eugenia disappeared into the train and didn't look back. The twinkling stars blanketed the night sky as Megan, James, Olivia, and Brya waved good-bye.

Brya no sooner recovered from putting her grandparents on the train than she was faced with saying good-bye to her child. As she lifted Olivia up, Brya wondered how she could be doing this to her own daughter. She looked into Olivia's innocent face and realized that this tiny being had no idea that she wouldn't be seeing her mama for some time. Brya sobbed. Olivia was too little to understand why her mama was crying. It was probably better that way.

When Brya reached inside her purse for a handkerchief, she pulled out one hundred dollars of the five hundred and handed it to Megan.

"Please use this for Olivia. I'll be sending you more when I get a little ahead. It'll help offset some of her expenses." Megan tried to give the money back.

"No, Megan, this is my rainy day money, and that day is here." Her sister didn't push the issue any further.

"Olivia," Brya said, as she held her daughter for the last time, "you mean the world to me, and one day, I'm going to give my little princess the moon and the stars." Brya pointed up to the circular, orange pie in the sky. Olivia giggled as she reached up and tried to touch it. "I mean every word of that, pumpkin, I do!"

Brya clutched her little girl one more time, cried, and then reluctantly handed her over to Megan. Her sister and brother-in-law boarded the train leaving Brya alone, waving good-bye. As Olivia was about to disappear inside, she turned her face back to her mama and then up at the moon. Brya broke down and walked away crying, hoping that she hadn't made the biggest mistake of her life.

Santa Fe, New Mexico

At 7:30 in the morning, Brya awoke to the sound of a gunshot. Fooled by another bad dream. She was due at her new job by nine. An uneasy sleep plagued her all night, and it was difficult to wake up. But get up she did, because today was the first day of training at Nina Nicholson's. Since arriving in Santa Fe, her nightmares had not stopped. In fact, they had gotten worse and more frequent. Brya couldn't understand why. The new life here was supposed to stop the memories and the pain.

Brya stumbled into the kitchen to put on some strong coffee. Then she turned on the faucet for her morning bath. The night before, she had set her hair in pin curls and was anxious to see the outcome.

After she got out of the bath and dried herself off, she waited for the steam to clear and brushed out her hair. She pinned it up and liked the look. Slipping into a tan suit that hugged her figure, Brya took one last check in the mirror. She was pleased.

When Brya arrived promptly at nine, Mrs. Shepard greeted her at the door with a smile. She was a professional woman in her early fifties, with a flair for fashion. Her hair was swept up, but what made it so striking was that the top layer of her hair was gray and the underneath, a dark brown.

"Good morning, Mrs. Shepard, is Miss Nicholson here?"

"She'll be here shortly, dear. Nina attended a fund-raiser last evening, and she's running a little late. She asked me to get you acquainted with the product line."

At the first counter, Mrs. Shepard stopped. "Brya, you are to wear only Nina's cosmetics, perfumes and skin care products. This will sell them better."

"Yes, ma'am. Do I have to buy them?"

"Absolutely not. As long as you continue working for the company, Nina will supply you with complimentary products, but don't give any away to potential clients. Understood?"

"Yes, ma'am."

Just then, Nina Nicholson swept through the front door wearing a cherry red suit with gold accessories.

"Good morning, Miss Nicholson."

Nina didn't waste a moment. "My how chic you look, Brya. And I love your hair." She immediately sprang into action. "Mrs. Shepard, start on the mailers we have discussed, and I will take over from here."

"I look forward to working with you, Brya," said Mrs. Shepard as she left the main salon.

"Likewise, Mrs. Shepard." Nina went through her entire line with Brya, from basic skin care products to fragrances. Her makeup line was particularly interesting. The packaging was gold and two "N's" were formed using the bodies of black leopards. It didn't take long to get acquainted with the merchandise. However, Brya sprayed so many scents from Nina's "Crystal Leopard Collection," that she had a nasty headache by the end of the day.

"Remember," said Nina as she finished her first day with Brya, "I want you to wear sophisticated clothing, tailored but feminine. Also, my number one rule is that the customer is always right. If any of these rules are violated, you will lose your job."

"Yes, ma'am."

For the next week, Brya was Nina's shadow. The woman was amazing. She had a knack with people; she easily got them into the palm of her hand, and made certain that while they were in there, they spent plenty of money. It was nothing for her to sell five hundred dollars to a single customer. Brya hoped to do as well.

❦

Nervous and excited, Brya "graduated" into sales. Nina was anxious to see how she performed.

The clientele of the salon were rich vacationers from all parts of the country, from movie stars to oil men. Many of them bragged about making money off the poor folks who lost all they owned in the Depression. Slum landlords and oil tycoons they called themselves. Patch was right. Santa Fe, rich in mining and minerals, with its unique terrain, provided a Shangri-La for the wealthy. The women arrived coifed in the latest designer fashions. Their pampered fingers, arms and necks were dripping in jewels, while the men who escorted them came 'dressed to the nines' in alligator shoes and camel's hair coats.

Santa Fe, with its light and landscape, also drew a Bohemian crowd of artists and writers from all over the world.

Brya was caught up in the fantasy of it all. This place made her feel safe and secure, like Trinity.

Selling came easily to her. She loved that Nina told her, "You've got the beauty to attract, and the personality to trap." Brya found that she liked to help men pick out that special gift for their fiancé, spouse, or lover. She was amazed at how many purchased lavish presents that weren't for their wives, and reminded herself that it was none of her business. She just did her job.

The daytime was controllable, but the nights tormented her. With the loss of sleep, her once-dancing eyes had become impassive. Being far away from family, who could she turn to? Who could she trust to help her? What good were nice clothes and exhilarating work when she felt run-down all the time? Brya had to pull herself together. Not only for her sake but for Olivia's as well.

In two months, Brya was able to send money to Megan for Olivia's first birthday and for her care. They talked once a week on the phone, so her daughter could hear her voice. James and Megan were having a grand time with their little niece. She had managed to get tangled up in seaweed at the beach, and was afraid to be near the water. But Brya was sure that would pass. Olivia saw her first pelican swoop down to grab a fish. When she watched the sand crabs dart around, Megan said that Olivia chased them everywhere but couldn't catch one before it disappeared into the sand. Megan told Brya not to worry about Olivia. She was a happy little girl and appeared to have adjusted well to the change.

When spring came, the snow on the mesas melted. Nina invited Brya to a dinner party for the top politicians from New Mexico. Nina loved these affairs, and since the politicians spent a lot of money in her store, it was good business to attend.

Brya found a blue satin cocktail dress with matching shoes. Nina had introduced her to a woman who could copy designer dresses at an affordable price. On Brya's salary, this was a blessing. She piled her hair loosely on top of her head, and secured it with a rhinestone clip.

Nina picked up her protégé and together they flew down the bumpy mountain road in her kelly green roadster. As they approached the house, Brya asked, "Who does this incredible home belong to?"

"Allen Ryan, a very handsome senator." Nina winked and checked herself in the rearview mirror, making sure her lipstick wasn't smeared.

"Will there be lots of famous people here tonight?" Brya asked.

"Of course, honey, but don't you worry your pretty head. People will adore you. You're a wonderful representative for my company." Nina patted her leg, and they exited the car.

The view from where they were standing was breathtaking. The moon and the stars cast a glow over the coral-pink canyon below. The home, perched on the side of the mountain, was the most romantic place Brya had ever seen. Laughter came from inside as Mexican mariachi music filtered out into the night.

Inside, a Negro butler, dressed in a tuxedo, offered them each a glass of champagne. Nina grabbed two and gave one to Brya. She remembered back to her wedding night with Holden and how the champagne made her feel. She missed him. But Holden would have wanted her to make a new life for herself. She took a large sip of the bubbly liquid. It exploded in her throat, and landed warm in her stomach.

"You better not get carried away. You don't want to wake up, on your day off, with your first hangover, do you?" Nina teased.

Brya continued to drink anyway. She didn't care. Maybe the alcohol would help her sleep.

The living room took full advantage of the picturesque view through ceiling-to-floor windows. Overstuffed pieces of masculine, southwest furniture made it a man's house—strong and powerful.

In no time flat, eyes were on Brya. She was the subject of whispers. She knew that she created quite a stir with the men but did her best not to make the women jealous. Beatrice taught her how to always spend time in the women's groups, even if she found the men more interesting. Her mama had been very good at not alienating anyone. All of a sudden, the champagne began to take effect. Her cheeks felt hot, and it was easier to talk to people she didn't know.

Out of nowhere, she saw a tall, handsome gentleman surveying the crowd. When he saw Brya, he walked over and said hello. She was mesmerized by his intensity.

"Hello," she said. All six feet of him were to her liking. He had a firm handshake and the rugged good looks that Brya had always found irresistible.

"And what would your name be, young lady?" he asked. By now, Brya was a little tipsy.

"My name is Brya Hunter."

He gave her a big, campaign grin. "I'm Henry Buchanan, newly elected governor of New Mexico." Speechless, she couldn't believe that he was actually standing there, talking to her.

She sat her glass down on a small table so she wouldn't drop it on the tile floor. The governor's eyes stayed fixed on her.

"Do you live here in Santa Fe?" he asked.

"I've just moved here from Oklahoma to work for Nina Nicholson."

Together, they took a seat on a sofa. "I've known Nina for years, but she didn't tell me that she'd hired such a charming and beautiful young lady."

Brya blushed. "Is there a Mrs. Buchanan? If so, I would like to meet her."

"Yes, there is, but she doesn't like social functions anymore. I suppose the political arena has taken its toll on her."

"I'm sorry to hear that, Governor. I can't understand how anyone would ever get bored at these beautiful parties." Brya glanced around the room, taking in all its grandeur.

They talked for fifteen minutes more before the dinner bell rang.

"Would you like to join me?" Henry asked. She was honored. Nina was engaged in conversation with two senators at the other end of the table.

The long, Spanish table and chairs were heavy and dark against the pink adobe walls and Saltillo tile floors. In one corner, small cacti, bathed in soft light, surrounded a jagged boulder. A warm, romantic glow fell across the room.

Henry leaned over, inhaling a whiff of Brya's perfume. "A fatted calf has been butchered for this event, I hear."

"You mean they killed a cow just for this dinner?" she replied.

He chuckled. "Our host has a small ranch here in Santa Fe, where he raises his own cattle. How would you like to visit it sometime?"

With a full mouth, she nodded her head yes.

"May I have your phone number? I'd like to call you after I check my schedule."

Brya almost choked on her food and agreed. Her head was spinning like a top as they talked long into the evening. Maybe it was the champagne, but she could easily get used to this lifestyle.

❧

"Nina, Henry Buchanan is such a charming man," Brya remarked on the drive home.

"I noticed that he had eyes for you, but may I remind you what a powerful man he is here in this state. His wife, however, has become a recluse and never appears in public anymore. I used to send products to their home by personal courier, but Mrs. Buchanan no longer requests them. I'm concerned about you getting tangled up with him. He'll never leave his wife, and you'll be hurt. Whatever you decide to do, please be discreet."

Brya felt dazed and confused. She glanced at her wristwatch. It read 2:00 A.M.

"I understand what you've told me, Nina, and I certainly don't want to hurt myself or your business. But, I grew close to him so quickly. What do I do?"

"You're a beautiful, smart woman who's already had to make a lot of life decisions. I'm sure that you'll make a wise one here. My wish for you—after you've made me a lot of money—is that you'll marry a multimillionaire, then bring Olivia to Santa Fe and live happily ever after."

The champagne didn't help Brya sleep at all. In fact, she tossed and turned all night. Her life was changing very quickly. Thoughts about sleeping with someone again were beginning to come back. It had been a while now since Holden's death, and she missed a man's touch. And Henry was such a vibrant person. She rolled over on her pillow, staring out at the night sky and heard a barn owl hooting in the distance. This repetitive sound finally put her to sleep.

Not many days passed and the governor called. It was a stormy evening and Brya was curled up in front of the fireplace, reading a mystery.

"Hello, Brya, it's Henry Buchanan. I have an opening in my schedule this coming Saturday. How would you like to visit 'Rio Salado,' Allen's ranch?" He hoped she wouldn't turn him down.

"Sure, sure, that would be grand," she replied, trying her best to contain herself. "What time should I be ready?"

"My driver will pick you up at one o'clock, and I'll meet you there."

As they hung up, Brya's stomach was filled with butterflies and her mind was racing. Was she making a big mistake getting involved with a married man—let alone the governor of New Mexico? Her mind said one thing and her heart said another. What about Mrs. Buchanan? What happened in their marriage to make her want to close off to her husband?

These questions plagued Brya and kindled another nightmare. The persistent dreams had become hellish firestorms she couldn't put out. This time, she was back in Trinity, married to Henry, who was close friends with her daddy. She was Oklahoma royalty. As Henry and Brya made endless love on the daybed, Brya was interrupted by the creak of a door and a child watching. It was Olivia, standing there with outstretched hands. Delusional, Brya awoke to the sound of her own voice. "Don't worry Olivia, Mommy will come back for you, and you're finally going to have a daddy."

❦

The next week flew by, and it was Saturday, time to meet Henry. The warm spring sun caressed all of Santa Fe. Brya chose a peach sundress and tan walking shoes, cool and comfortable. She tied her hair back with a ribbon and added some blush and matching lipstick. As she was applying the finishing touches, there was a knock at her door.

A young, rosy-cheeked man in a chauffeur's uniform tipped his hat to her.

"Good morning. The governor has sent me to pick you up. Let me know when you're ready."

"One moment, please, while I get my purse."

She hopped into the backseat of a shiny, black Cadillac. A woman could get used to this.

"What's your name?" Brya asked, as she sank down in the black leather seat.

"Mike Nichols, ma'am. I'm the governor's chauffeur. I hope you enjoy the ride to the ranch."

"I'm new to the area and haven't seen much. Tell me about the local Indians." Brya felt sorry for them ever since her drive with Patch years ago.

"Well Miss Hunter, legend has it that the Navajo people believed that they were worms that climbed out of the earth and into this world. They are happy here and live on the mesa tops and rimrocks." He pointed to the Jemez Mountains and the Rowe Mesa to the west.

"They're so stark," Brya replied, not yet used to the unusual terrain.

"Yes, but during the Depression," he continued, "the Indians were some of the best survivors because they could live on very little and trade for the rest of what they needed."

Elk bread, turquoise mining, evil spirits, and bleached bones entertained her on the rest of the drive.

Before she knew it, Brya was at the gate of "Rancho del Rio Salado," nestled in the heart of the great Rio Grande Valley. The rushing waters of the winding Rio Grande had nourished the Pueblo Indians for centuries. Rio Salado was a sight straight out of a fairy tale.

When they arrived, Henry was waiting—beaming from head to toe—and looking as though he owned the place. He wore rough-out boots, and his chambray shirt, open at the neck, exposed a lean, muscled chest with a touch of gray hair.

"You are a sight for sore eyes," he said as he turned Brya around admiring her dress. "You're prettier than when I first met you."

She blushed as he took her hand and escorted her around the ranch. "Where is everyone?" she asked.

"Allen is on a business trip to Washington D.C., but his staff will tend to our needs. Your only job is to enjoy yourself."

Allen's mainstay was his Longhorn cattle. He kept a couple of Palomino ponies for his private use, and several cowboys tended to the herd.

As they strolled through the ranch house, Brya admired Allen's collection of Indian Kachinas, ancient tribal bowls, and old jewelry.

The butler entered with some drinks. "Would you like to try one?" Henry asked. He handed her a concoction filled with tomato juice and a large celery stick.

"What's this?"

"It's a Bloody Mary. It just might wet your whistle on a hot day and help you relax, too." She gingerly sipped it and enjoyed the spicy bite.

Her hope was that it wouldn't be too strong, or else she'd lose her inhibitions.

"Tell me about yourself, Brya," Henry said. "You have such mysterious qualities."

"You don't want to know about me, Henry. You're the governor of New Mexico. I'm sure you have more stories to tell than I do."

Henry didn't waste any time in talking. Brya was glad because she didn't want to dredge up all her memories.

"I'm fifty-six years old, and have two daughters about your age. Our family was poor, but close. My father worked hard as a blacksmith in Montana to get me through school. Just like the metals he hammered, he molded me into shape. When I was old enough to work, I put myself through law school. One thing led to another and now I'm governor. I've always worked hard, and I respect the value of a dollar."

"Tell me about your wife," Brya said, as she placed her drink on the coffee table. "It may be none of my business, but I'm curious. After all, you're here with me while she sits at home."

"Laurel is one of the most beautiful women I've ever known. You remind me of her. She used to be so vivacious, but one day she just stopped going out and closed her legs to me. I'll always love her; she's the mother of my children. But the woman I once knew is gone."

Brya looked long and hard into his sad eyes and believed him, especially since Nina had spoken to her about it already.

He took her face in his hands. "Excuse me for being so abrupt, but when I first saw you, you took my breath away. You're warm, interesting and bright. I want you in my life, Brya." Before she knew it, he reached inside his shirt pocket and brought out a present.

She opened the package and found a gold bracelet with one brilliant diamond in the middle. "Henry," she gasped, "you don't even know me! You shouldn't have given me this. I can't take it." She tried to hand it back but he refused to accept it.

"I want you to have it because we do know each other; there was chemistry between us the moment we met. I feel as though I've known you all my life, and I challenge you to tell me that's not true."

She couldn't deny it.

He placed the bracelet around her tiny wrist, admiring the brilliance of the diamond.

Brya was caught up in the moment. Ever since she was a little girl, she had appreciated beautiful things. It had been a long time since anyone had given her a gift. Her mama and daddy would not have approved of a relationship with a married man, but would be proud that she had attracted such a powerful individual. Maybe she'd even be the governor's wife some day.

His hand slid softly across her shoulder, gently pulling her close. Brya tried to ignore her feelings but the attraction was more than she could handle.

They kissed and fondled each other until kissing was not enough.

"Come with me," Henry whispered.

It had been too long for either of them. He pulled back strands of hair from her face, then undressed her. She was as beautiful as he had envisioned. His soft hands swept over her breasts like a gentle wind while his tongue made her cry out for more.

"I want all of you, Brya." His intense eyes hungered, and spoke a silent language that she understood. He placed her perfect form on top, and she arched as he slid deep inside her. Their two bodies writhed in unison as their search came to an end.

Mike showed up at 7:30 that evening to take her home. It was hard for Brya to leave.

"I've enjoyed myself more than you could ever know, Brya, and I will be in touch very soon," Henry said.

She didn't say a word but looked up at him with dreamy eyes, twirling her new bracelet on her wrist. They shared a long kiss good-bye before she headed outside. The smell of wood smoke danced on the wind. Rio Salado, Brya secretly hoped, would continue to be their rendezvous spot.

For a few months, Brya lived in a fairy tale world, but the demands on her time weighed heavily on her mind. The relationship with Henry overlapped with her long hours at work and numerous appearances at society functions.

She had made only one trip to see her daughter. Brya hoped that periodic phone calls would suffice. How was she to balance the hectic work schedule, Henry's needs, and more frequent visits to see Olivia? There weren't enough hours in a day. Her grandparents were still fighting gout and arthritis. They would call her at work, but she hardly had the time to talk with them.

Long days turned into longer, sleepless nights.

During one day at the salon, Nina couldn't help but notice the dark circles underneath Brya's eyes. "You're looking a little worse for wear lately. Is everything all right?"

"I'm just a little tired, Nina," Brya replied, studying herself in a cosmetic mirror. "I haven't been sleeping well for months."

"I know how it is, dear. But when you have the busy schedule that we have, sometimes you need something to help you sleep. I will let you in on my little secret."

Brya was intrigued.

Nina reached into her purse and handed her a bottle. "Take one of these before bed, and you'll be relaxed and off to sleep before you know it. If they do the trick, keep the bottle."

"Thank you," Brya replied, studying the contents.

"You probably need some time off, too. Why don't you go visit your daughter? Consider it a paid vacation."

Brya sat down on a stool, at a loss for words. Olivia had been a neglected chapter in her life. To see her now meant writing her back in.

❦

When it was time to board the plane at the Albuquerque airport, Brya mused that it looked like a fat, silver bird with shiny wings. She settled in her seat, organized Olivia's gifts in the overhead bin, and braced herself for the takeoff.

As she laid her head against the headrest, she thought about Henry. It bothered her that she couldn't be seen with him in public. And he made her vow not to talk to anyone about their relationship.

She was lonely for companionship. Would she be the one he would leave his wife for? He had not made any promises. If she could live in the governor's mansion, Olivia would be well taken care of, just like she had been in the Great House. Her mama once told her that no one needed to tell her how to get something. Brya would figure out a way to win Henry.

In no time at all, Brya landed in Los Angeles and James, Megan, and Olivia were there to greet her. Olivia was now one and a half years old and looked like a little cherub. Her thick, auburn hair framed her rosy cheeks. Pinchable, chubby rolls layered her legs and arms. A doctor told Megan that Olivia would be tall and big-boned. It appeared that Brya and Olivia would never look anything alike.

Megan knelt down to Olivia and pointed to Brya, but the child just stared at the strange woman walking toward her, then turned to hang on to Megan.

"I just spoke with you last night, sweetheart," Brya said, reaching her arms out to her daughter. Olivia studied her for a moment, not sure what to think.

"I've brought presents for you." Brya pulled out a bright red package from her bag and dangled it in front of her. "Come here, angel."

The child looked at the gift, then her mother, and finally walked over to her.

Brya gave her a big hug and handed her the present. Olivia stayed in her arms, trying to figure out what was inside, but she still paid no attention to her mother. Megan and James watched with worried looks, but then rallied. "Santa Fe must be doing all the right things for you because you look great."

No reply. Brya remembered her grandpa's words years ago. "You are only trying to provide Olivia with a caring home until you are able to take care of yourself again." Today she questioned if she could ever take care of herself enough to be a mother. She felt like a cuckoo who left its eggs in another bird's nest to raise.

Olivia sat beside Brya in the backseat on the drive through the San Fernando Valley.

"Here, let me help you open it, you silly goose," Brya said. Olivia babbled and grinned.

The sound of her daughter's voice was refreshing.

Olivia pretended to help as Brya unwrapped a miniature pony made of real horse's hair, complete with a hand-tooled bridle and saddle. Olivia's eyes got as big as saucers as Brya pranced it across her lap, whinnying like a horse.

Olivia whooped in delight as her mother rubbed the horsehair, first pushing it one way, then the other. Brya and Olivia played "horsie" all the way to the farm, and Brya forgot to look out at Los Angeles, California.

As Brya stepped out of the car onto the driveway of the small farm, the smell of citrus overtook her.

Megan proudly explained that they had about two hundred and fifty orange and lemon trees. The following day, in the daylight, she'd show Brya the grove.

Olivia and her mother played endlessly until they both collapsed on the floor—and by bedtime, they had successfully reacquainted themselves.

The child's bedroom was fit for a princess. It was decorated as if she lived inside the sea, full of dolphins and seals. The rug resembled the ocean, complete with seaweed, sea horses, sand dollars, and clams. Olivia pointed to every one of them. After Brya put her daughter into bed, her mind drifted back to the days at the Great House, when she and her sisters were being tucked in by her mama and daddy. Then she remembered the last night that her brothers and sisters spent together in their house, and loneliness swept over her again.

Brya tucked the comforter tightly around her daughter's chin and kissed her forehead. "I love you, my angel. You have no idea how much I miss you." As Brya started to leave the bedroom, she reached down to turn on the night-light. Olivia began to cry and Brya saw confusion in her eyes. Who was she crying for, her Aunt Megan or her?

Brya began stroking her head to calm her down. "Sweetheart, listen to Mommy. I haven't left you. You are better off staying with Aunt Megan. She can take care of you better than I can right now."

Olivia continued to cry and Brya didn't know what to do, so she kept talking. "Honey, you will come to live with Mommy real soon. Don't fret, Olivia. Everything's going to be just fine, you'll see. Now, get some sleep, little darlin', because we have a big day tomorrow."

Brya kissed her daughter on the forehead, and slowly left the room, leaving Olivia to cry herself to sleep in her ocean paradise.

A troubled Megan took her sister to the upstairs loft near her daughter's bedroom. The evening had worn Brya out and she needed to sleep . . . and escape. Nina's pills had become her best friend.

❦

Megan couldn't sleep and woke up before anyone. Brya slept in late due to the effect of the sleeping pill. There was so much to talk about over coffee and pastries. Brya noticed that her sister had gained weight, in part, she thought because she was happy, but mostly because she loved to eat fattening food.

As they sipped their coffee, Brya, still groggy, looked out of the kitchen windows, admiring the bright, sunny day and the grove in the back yard. So many flowers grew in

California—colors and shapes that she had never seen before. Megan seemed restless and fidgety.

"You obviously like Santa Fe, Brya, because you have hardly visited your daughter," Megan snapped.

"I do like Santa Fe, Megan, but that's not why I haven't come to visit more often. It's my job—so demanding and all. I can't just get up and leave whenever I feel like it." Brya couldn't mention Henry.

"I understand that you need to make a new life for yourself but you need to get over your past losses. I'm concerned that you and Olivia are not living together. And on top of that, I'm pregnant," she said curtly, patting her stomach and reaching for another piece of apple strudel.

"Oh sis, I'm so excited. How far along are you?"

"Brya, don't change the subject. Your life has taken on such a new twist that there's no longer room for Olivia in it."

Brya, still dazed, had no comeback.

"Don't get me wrong. Olivia is a delight, and we don't mind taking care of her. We love children, so it won't be a hardship to have her with us when the baby comes. But, she's your daughter. What are your plans for taking her back?"

"Sis, I'm working hard to create some security for Olivia and me. I don't want her to go through things like I did. When I have a nice home and a husband, I'll be able to take her back. Right now, I not only work full-time, but Nina also requires me to socialize with our clientele. It'll hurt Olivia worse to be there and have me ignore her."

"But Brya . . ."

"No Megan, let me finish. To be honest, right now, I don't have a clue as to when I can bring her back."

Megan tried to argue but got nowhere with her sister, who was adamant in her belief that Olivia must not come back until she married a rich husband.

"Brya, you're making the biggest mistake of your life." Megan got up, knocking her coffee cup on the floor, and stormed out of the room.

❦

The week went by too quickly for Brya. She was unable to make up with Megan so that things were like they used to be. This made her uneasy. Megan was the most family she had. Now she had to go back to Santa Fe. Brya had grown so attached to her daughter that leaving her behind was painful.

When it was time for her to board the plane, no one said a word. Megan was obviously holding back her feelings. After Brya gave Olivia her final hug and kiss, she turned to go and heard a teary little voice cry out, "Mama."

Reality and Fantasy

It was 1939. The city of San Francisco glistened like Turkish jewels in the moonlight.

In the 1860s it had been a wide-open town full of prostitution and gambling—back alleys of irrefutable deeds and lust. Here it was easy to disappear.

This dazzling den of iniquity became another rendezvous spot for Henry and Brya. Under assumed names at the Fairmont Hotel on Nob Hill, they participated in the unscrupulous rituals of the city.

Henry provided an island of ripe adventure: exotic restaurants, private yachts, expensive wines, and French lingerie.

The yachts were Brya's favorite, so Henry indulged her. He got more of what he wanted that way. They had spent years of incredible intensity at Allen's ranch, but liaisons on the California coast were rare and exciting.

❦

The sailboat undulated like a sensual Latin dance. Naked, Brya and Henry sipped brandy by candlelight, falling into each other to the rhythm of the sea. He liked to listen to her scream and see her arch on top of him as they rose and fell together.

On one such evening, Henry raised himself slightly and looked at Brya's delicate face. Her perfect features stood out against the flicker of a nearby candle. His hand never stopped stroking her soft, damp belly.

"You're the only woman for me," he whispered. "I've come alive since I met you. Be mine, forever, Brya."

Her heart raced. She had waited for so long to hear these words. She kissed him softly on the lips. "I love you, Henry. I can't wait until we can finally be together."

"Me too, angel. Me too." He kissed her back, and reached over to pull out a small box from his shirt pocket.

"I have something special for my girl."

She knew it was a ring, she just knew it.

"Open it, Brya." Henry stroked her shoulders and held her close.

Her hands tore into the tiny box and pulled out a two-carat diamond ring. She immediately placed it on her left hand, admiring the facets.

"Do you like it?" he asked.

"Like it? I love it! Does this mean that we're . . ."

Henry hesitated, then ran his hand through her golden hair. "Yes, Brya. I intend to leave Laurel, as soon as I can see my way clear. But it could take a while because a divorce from her could be nasty. Let's just call it an unofficial engagement."

Brya's eyes welled up with tears. She threw her arms around Henry's neck and smothered him with kisses. He was hers at last.

❦

The opulent ways of the wealthy were in Brya's blood. After all, if her family's money and prestige had not been ripped out from underneath her, she would have been royalty—Oklahoma royalty. No one could rob her of that pedigree. It was nice to be treated like a princess again, just like her daddy did.

Brya was on top of the world. Her sales at Nina Nicholson's had hit an all-time high, making her self-esteem immeasurable. No longer a young vulnerable girl, she had carved out a sufficient life for herself. Time had changed her, partly due to the relationship with Henry, but mostly because of all her losses. Hardened by life's disappointments, she had become clever and tough. After all, she had landed the governor of New Mexico.

Henry enjoyed this captivating young woman. She entertained him and added spice to his life. Brya was a charming conversationalist and a masterful artist in the bedroom. What more could a man ask for?

Just one thing gnawed at her—Olivia. Brya was pulled into two different directions: reality and fantasy.

The reality was that she had avoided being a parent. It took soul, and her heart and soul left the day she saw her daddy die. Until she put this behind her, she couldn't truly love again. Brya couldn't give what she didn't have. It wasn't her fault, it had been enough for her to survive these past fourteen years.

The fantasy was that she would successfully pull her daughter into a rich world with a new father. The good life would heal all their wounds.

❧

The next morning, Fisherman's Wharf was particularly quiet except for the sound of hungry seagulls crying through the clouds. The smell of fish suffocated the ocean air. Henry had some urgent business to take care of, so Brya decided to take a walk. It was a chilly summer day. The choppy waters of the San Francisco Bay lapped endlessly against the wharf. Brya tightened her jacket around her neck and strolled the pier staring at the fishermen reeling in their catch. A bedraggled lady of the evening walked by on her way home and disappeared into an alley. In the distance loomed Alcatraz Island, a living hell for criminals of the worst kind.

Brya sat down on a nearby bench clutching a cup of hot coffee, and admiring her new ring. Memories of her childhood seeped back into her consciousness. As she stared at the gray walls of Alcatraz, she realized that she had lived in a prison of deaths and losses. Freedom had become precious when it was taken away.

Henry had filled Brya with hope and joy for the future. The prospect of escaping her past was imminent. Like a released prisoner, she was free, stronger than ever, and able to accept Olivia into her life.

She finished her coffee, tossing the paper cup into a trash can, and focused her attention on the here and now.

She passed a small diner where a group of people were gathered around the radio with concerned looks on their faces. Curious, Brya walked in. Germany had invaded Poland and there was talk of war. She must find Henry.

The Rape

Brya's hopes ran high. Henry would divorce Laurel to marry her. After six years, she and Olivia were going to be able to live in the governor's mansion, where they belonged. The wait was worth the sacrifices.

Zozobra, a forty-foot paper maché boogieman, towered above the Santa Fe crowd. Both the hideous figure and the governor kicked off the week-long celebration of "Fiesta" each year.

Zozobra, a harmless marionette, moaned and groaned, twisted his head, and flailed his arms in frustration. Like a dragon, fire spewed out of his empty head which burned him to the ground in order to devour all bad fortune.

Brya sat wide-eyed. Every year, the same ritual lit up the night sky the weekend following Labor Day. The plaza was teaming with fiesta-goers. Spanish dancers whirled in a flurry of ruffles and sparkling trinkets as mariachi music filled the night. Candlelight processions went by, looking like rivers of white diamonds.

Brya, obsessed with Henry, watched him like a hawk as he mingled with the crowd. It was torture not to be able to be with him. Her stomach churned as other ladies vied for his attention.

She was not anxious to talk to anyone after getting over a lingering cold. Eager to get out, she roamed through the plaza nibbling on a tamale.

Suddenly, a deep, Texas voice interrupted her thoughts, "Why, who do we have here, you pretty little thing?"

Startled, Brya dropped her food, turned, and looked up under a white Stetson hat.

"Who wants to know?" she replied.

"I'm Brandon Cole Harrison III, ma'am. Nice to make your acquaintance."

"What brings you to Santa Fe, Mr. Harrison?"

"Call me Cole, darlin'."

"*Cole*," Brya said sarcastically.

"Why you're just a little spitfire, aren't ya?"

"Why are you here, *Cole*?"

"Oil, darlin'. I'm drillin' a well just outside of town." Brya's eyes lit up—an oil man. "Besides, I'm Henry Buchanan's campaign manager. Without my money, he wouldn't be governor."

This man seemed awfully full of himself, she thought. And why has Henry never mentioned him?

"Do you live here?" he asked.

"Yes, I do."

"A pretty lady like you is probably married."

"No, are you?" She had moved her engagement ring to the other hand so no one would ask any questions.

"Well, I'm engaged to a wild thing back in Texas but I just couldn't help but admire some local Santa Fe beauty."

"Nice to meet you, Mr. Harrison. Have a good trip back." Brya walked away.

"Little lady, you never gave me your name," he yelled, admiring the wiggle in her walk.

Much to his dismay, she disappeared into the crowd. Somehow he'd find out who she was.

What a pompous man, she thought. She felt a chill and buttoned her sweater, eager to go home. As she meandered her way through the plaza, admiring the wares, she heard a familiar voice behind her. It was Henry, talking to a man she had not seen before. Henry did not see her.

"Listen to me, Henry," the man said. "The cancer has spread to her brain. You have about one month to spend with your wife before she dies. You must give up everything to be with her. I'm advising you, not only as a doctor, but as a friend. This move will only make you look better in the public eye."

Brya felt sick. She couldn't believe what she was hearing.

"All right, doctor. I'll have my secretary adjust my schedule so that I can be home to take care of her. If only she had never gotten this terrible disease, we would have been together forever."

❧

Brya was crushed. Six years for nothing. Her head started spinning.

The doctor patted Henry on the shoulder and left.

Enraged, she seized the opportunity to confront this liar.

"Henry Buchanan, I want a word with you!" Brya snapped.

Henry wheeled around in shock. "I told you never to speak to me in public."

"To hell with your image. You've ruined six years of my life."

"What do you mean?" he said innocently.

"I felt sorry for you with your reclusive wife, when all along, she had a dreadful disease. Instead of staying home and taking care of her, you were sleeping with me all over Santa Fe and San Francisco."

"A man has to get his needs met, Brya, and you were perfect—young and naïve."

She slapped him, feeling anger like she never had before. "You never intended to marry me, did you?"

He said nothing. Henry's veins were bulging out of his neck as he tried his best not to lose control.

"What did you plan on doing with me after Laurel died?"

Henry grabbed her arm and pulled her behind an empty booth. "I didn't mean what I said a minute ago about getting my needs met. I sincerely want to marry you. But I have to wait a while after Laurel's funeral. It would affect my image to have the governor marry so early."

"You're such a liar. From the very beginning you led me on with no intention of marrying again."

"But Brya, listen . . ."

"Before I go, Henry, just answer me one question: why the lavish gifts, but no money?"

Brya had his number, and Henry was furious that he didn't get his way. "I gave you gifts so you wouldn't feel like a whore. Besides, some of them were presents that I had given Laurel which she could no longer enjoy."

"Was the ring hers, too?" Brya shouted.

Henry wouldn't look at her.

She struck him again and spun around, pushing her way through the gaping crowd, leaving him in the public eye where he belonged.

Brya's heart ached as she ran down the dirt road. Tears clouded her vision as she fought her way through the night to her front door.

"I don't want to be alone!" she cried out, throwing herself on the bed. She sobbed as minutes turned into hours.

Then, it was as if a puppeteer lifted Brya up and brought her to life. "I'm not alone. I have a daughter who loves me."

She calmly took off the ring and placed it in her jewelry box. She would sell it, and use the money for Olivia's birthday present.

❦

Overcome with sadness, Brya looked forward to her pills. But the night had no mercy. She thrashed her covers trying to avoid the scream of the demons.

She and Olivia were connected by an umbilical cord, set apart by a long series of mahogany doors with beveled glass, but Brya couldn't reach her. Olivia was playing in a yard full of toys and stuffed animals. One by one, Brya opened each door, frantic and getting nowhere. Suddenly, Megan appeared, holding a giant pair of scissors, and laughed hysterically as she cut the cord. "You've lost your daughter for good. She's mine," Megan shouted as she and Olivia disappeared into the mist.

Brya, jarred awake by the shrieking sound of a whistling train, telephoned the airline. Nina would understand; she needed to see her daughter.

❦

"Happy birthday to you, happy birthday to you, happy birthday, dear Olivia . . . happy birthday to you!!" Olivia blew out all seven candles on her chocolate cake, and a huge smile spread over her face as Megan and James passed out paper plates to all of Olivia's friends. Brya watched the children clamor for the double rich cake and vanilla ice cream. Megan's little boy, Jimmy, now almost six years old, kept trying to stick his plate up for dessert until Olivia finally handed him one.

Brya had flown in the night before Olivia's birthday, drawn and jittery. Her use of sleeping pills and alcohol couldn't hide the deep pain inside. She had made a mistake by not putting her daughter first, and hoped to be able to make it through this visit without having to defend herself, once again, to her sister. She gave Olivia a sizable check as a present. She was no longer sure what her daughter liked.

This way, they could spend a day shopping, just the two of them.

While Brya watched Olivia interact with her friends, she noticed that her daughter had blossomed into a beautiful young girl, who looked more like an adolescent with long legs than the little girl she really was. Her wavy, brown hair cascaded well below her shoulders. Someday soon, Brya would put her in one of Nina's luxurious baths, in the same way Mama Beatrice used to do for Brya.

After the party guests had gone home, Megan and Brya glanced around at the mess.

"Let's send Olivia and Jimmy out to play, Brya," Megan said, rubbing the aching sides of her back.

"Great idea. We have a lot of work to do."

Jimmy was smaller than most boys his age but definitely cute, with big blue eyes and a freckled, turned up nose. He wore his parents out because he needed to be busy with something new every five minutes. Olivia helped Megan handle the rambunctious little boy, just like an older sister.

Olivia grabbed Jimmy's grubby hand and they shot out the back door toward the neighboring cornfield. As Brya watched them, they quickly became swallowed up by the tall, green stalks of corn. This made her uneasy. She couldn't pick them out among the changing colors of the rows, and noticed that parked further ahead in the distance, along the edge of the cornfield, was a black pickup truck with what looked like two men inside. Brya remembered James commenting on the fact that the neighbors often hired migrant workers to tend their crops. She looked back to the cornfield but could not see any sign of Olivia and Jimmy. Brya tossed her apron on the kitchen table and raced out the door as she yelled to Megan that she was going to check on the children.

Brya ran down the dirt path that bordered the corn. She could hear the children laughing, playing hide-and-seek, but still couldn't see them. The men in the truck must have heard them, too, because they were watching. Their faces were turned toward Brya and she could see that they were dark-skinned Mexican men.

"You can't find me!" Olivia shouted. Just then both children ran out of the cornfield. The two men looked at Olivia and their eyes traveled up and down her body. Completely unaware, Olivia ran over to the truck and squatted beside it. As Jimmy ran around from the other side of the truck, she touched him, yelling, "I got you!"

Brya ran up to the vehicle ready to get them both home. A voice from inside the truck said, "Buenos dias." The children jumped and Olivia walked over to see who was talking to them.

"Olivia," Brya shouted, "run home now. And take Jimmy with you. Go!"

The girl ignored her mother but Jimmy ran into the bushes, alarmed by the panic in Brya's voice.

"Niña," the driver said, leering at her, "Le gusta dulce?" He dangled a Hershey bar in front of her.

Olivia took a step back, staring at the grinning Mexican men.

Brya dashed over to Olivia, grabbing her arm. "Olivia, I said get out of here!"

"He just wants to give me candy, Mother," said the child as she tore away from her grip. "Besides, you never give me anything!"

Before Brya had a chance to react, the driver threw open the door and jumped out, grabbing her arms and slapping her around. He pulled out a stiletto and flicked it in her face, shouting, "Callate la boca estupida puta o te corto la cara!" Brya knew enough Spanish to understand that he called her a stupid whore and wanted to cut her face.

"No, not my face!" she cried out. "It's all I have!"

"Callate!" he shouted, as she struggled in his arms.

Brya knew that if her face was scarred, the dream of marrying a rich man would be severed, and she and Olivia would have nothing. His alcohol breath made her gag as he pressed the sharp blade deeper into her skin. Brya was not strong enough to fight him. Olivia tried to pull him off her mother, but wasn't strong enough either.

The other man on the passenger side got out of the truck—his dirty hand holding his bulging groin. Brya writhed and strained, trying to get loose from her attacker. The passenger grabbed the chocolate bar from the seat of the truck and tried to hand it to Olivia. She knocked it away and tried to hit the driver who held a knife to her mother. Her cotton dress had climbed up her legs, exposing a touch of her pink panties—and that was all it took.

The passenger jumped out of the truck, grabbed Olivia, and pinned her down to the ground. He ripped off her panties, and in front of her mother, quickly undid his pants, eager to rape Brya's little girl. Brya screamed and tried to fight her way free, but the man holding the knife to her face choked her so hard she couldn't breathe. Then he threw her on the ground, hitting her several times, and cut open her clothes with his knife. She closed her eyes knowing that she too was going to be raped. Olivia cried out. "Mommy, Aunt Megan, help me. I need you!"

Brya looked over at her daughter. Her child was bleeding from her vagina, her face twisted with pain. Brya thought she heard the bushes rustle. Was it Jimmy?

Olivia's desperate attempts to fight failed, and now the man forced his huge penis into her small mouth. The look on her face was of total horror, as he forced her head up and down. The overwhelming stench of urine-soaked underwear, dirt, and sweat, made her gag. As he moaned and groaned on top of her, Olivia bit him. He slapped her. She tried again, but this time he punched her so hard that he knocked her out, and could perform whatever act he wanted, without interruption. He tossed her around like a rag doll, violating every part of the young girl's body.

Olivia lay unconscious in the dirt. Her assailant got up, zipped his pants and smeared some vaginal blood from his hands on the upholstery of his truck, grinning and satisfied. Then the driver picked Brya up by her shoulders and threw her to the side, finished, and walked away as if nothing had happened. The two men drove off.

Brya's naked body throbbed with pain, and her face hurt from being hit. She touched it—grateful that there were no cuts. She then crawled over to Olivia, picked her up, and began rocking her limp and battered body.

"Oh God!" she cried. "Why has all this happened to me? Why? Why? What have I done wrong?"

Olivia's eyes were wide open and fixed on the sky. Her mother couldn't rouse her. She frantically tried to rearrange Olivia's dress, smearing the blood and semen with her trembling hands—the same way she had done on her dress the day her daddy died.

"Oh God. My baby girl. Olivia!" Brya's mind was racing with guilt. "This whole thing is my fault; my daughter is worse than dead. Her life has been ruined." Brya wailed in pain.

Jimmy, Megan and James came running. Megan became hysterical as soon as she saw Olivia, and fell on her knees next to her, crying.

"Brya, what happened to my Olivia? You can't even be a mother for one afternoon," Megan screamed. "What have you done!?"

For the first time in Brya's life, she was defenseless. As she stared at Olivia's bruised and tender face, it was hard to admit that she had done nothing for her daughter, not now, and not for the past six years. As a mother, she was a failure.

"Megan," James said calmly, "please. We need to get them both to the hospital. Help me."

James took off his shirt and put it around Brya's shoulders. Next, he scooped Olivia's limp body into his arms. Megan pulled down her blood-stained dress and smoothed her hair. She then carefully collected Brya's tattered clothes and helped her sister to her feet. They headed home to call the doctor. The two assailants were probably over the border by now, never to be seen again. Calling the police seemed pointless.

As soon as they reached the kitchen, Megan called Dr. Strauss. He would meet them at Valley General.

Megan got clothes for Brya while James wrapped Olivia in a blanket. They rushed out the door to get Olivia to the hospital, and Brya followed in silence.

The Cover-up

Olivia was whisked into the emergency ward as soon as they arrived. She was still in shock. A nurse escorted Brya to a room where a doctor examined her and a strong sedative was administered. She immediately fell into a deep sleep, the first one in months.

Later, while still in a muddled state, she telephoned Nina to explain what had happened. A family emergency was easy for her to understand and Brya was to take as much time as she needed.

She lay back and breathed a sigh of relief. Suddenly, Megan entered the room, obviously disturbed and set for battle. "We need to talk. You never told me what happened out there today."

Brya wasn't ready for combat. The pill was her commanding officer. She spoke methodically. "I was forced to watch my daughter get raped." A single tear made its way down her swollen cheek. "Promise me that you won't breathe a word of this to anyone, ever. If this leaks out, it will ruin me. I know better than anyone how to handle this."

Megan couldn't believe what she was hearing.

"You have a daughter lying in a hospital bed who was just raped. And all you can think about is *yourself*? You've turned into a monster! What has happened to you?"

Brya's battered eyes bored through her sister like a steel drill. "You don't know what it's like to suffer. I saw our daddy shoot himself, not you. It was me that was covered in his brains and blood. I had twin babies die at birth and I never got to hold them. I was the one who had to watch the only man who ever really loved me die. You know nothing about what it's like to lose everything you ever loved!"

Just then, James arrived after spending a long time discussing the assault with Dr. Strauss. He had overheard the fight and felt like he was walking into a minefield.

"Brya," he said, trying to ignore the tenseness in the room, "be prepared when you see Olivia because it's not a pretty sight. She just lies in her bed, staring at the ceiling. The only good news is that the doctor believes she will heal, physically. The rapist didn't ruin her reproductive organs."

For a brief moment, Brya envied Olivia. Her daughter had ruined her chance of having more children. But Brya's pride took over and she maintained decorum. "Everything will be fine. There is nothing that the two of us can't work out together." James had no response and walked away.

Megan, still fuming from their argument, cursed the day she asked Brya to take Olivia back home. Her sister wasn't capable of taking care of herself, let alone a child.

Megan and James left to get some food. Now was a good time for Brya to visit Olivia, alone.

It hurt for Brya to get out of bed. Her feet hit the cold floor, and she walked slowly toward Olivia's room.

Brya stopped suddenly. Room 204—the same room number she had when she lost her baby boys. She felt like throwing up as a wave of nausea came over her. She held on to the door jam and looked into the room.

Olivia lay quietly in the bed, staring into space. Several bandages covered her head and arms. She didn't move, just like James had said. The sickness in Brya's stomach increased, remembering what had happened. She walked to her and lightly touched her small shoulder, then placed a kiss on the one part of her head that was not bandaged.

"Olivia." No response. "Olivia, it's Mother. I'm here, honey."

Olivia didn't move.

"Sweetheart, please? Speak to me."

Olivia rolled her head to one side and winced. Her right ear was badly discolored. It must have hurt just to move. Then Olivia looked straight at her mother. Brya would never forget the look on her daughter's face. All her rage and suffering were directed at her mother. In that one look, she communicated their future.

Brya trembled as she sat on the chair next to Olivia's bed. Tears ran down her cheeks. "Honey, you must be in terrible pain. Isn't there anything I can do for you?"

"No, I'm not in pain!" Olivia clutched her abdomen and glared, her bloodshot eyes full of anger. "Why did you let that Mexican hurt me? Why didn't you stop him?" Olivia's eyes darted back and forth groping for a response.

Brya chose her words carefully. "Olivia, I tried to pull you away but you wouldn't listen. Then, before I knew it, it was too late. You saw the other man grab me. He was too strong. There was nothing that I could do with a knife against my face. I felt so helpless."

"You love your face more than me," Olivia shouted. "You told the Mexican that was all you had."

Brya didn't remember saying that.

"Olivia, you've had a horrible thing happen to you, and you're not yourself right now. I love you more than anything, darling. I've been working very hard to try and build a better life for us. Please don't push me away. I realize you're upset but please, please understand that I'm here to help you make all of this go away."

Olivia mustered up enough strength to raise up on one elbow. The sunlight from the window fell on her pulverized face, exposing the purple bruises. Her hair was matted with dried blood.

"You always left me, Mommy. You don't love me. Go away! Go away! I hate you!"

The nurse came running. "What's going on here? Can't you see you're upsetting my patient?"

"But nurse . . ."

"If Olivia is upset by you," the nurse interrupted, "then I suggest you leave immediately."

"Excuse me, I'm Olivia's mother," Brya replied, fighting for her position. "She's just experiencing a nasty reaction to what happened to her. I'm going to stay until she calms down."

The nurse didn't budge. "Do I need to call the doctor?"

Brya reluctantly picked up her purse and took one last glance at her daughter. "I do love you, Olivia. Please forgive me."

"I want Aunt Megan! I want Aunt Megan!" she screamed.

As Brya was escorted out of the room, she felt as though she had been stabbed in the heart, twice. First Henry and now her daughter. Megan was coming down the long hallway with some fruit.

"How did it go with Olivia?"

"It didn't go well at all." Tears welled up in Brya's eyes. "She wants you, Megan."

"You can't blame her, can you?"

Leaving her dignity intact, Brya asked James to check her out of the hospital and take her home to rest.

Megan relished getting in the last words. "You don't mind if I spend the night with Olivia, do you?"

Before Brya had a chance to respond, James interjected.

"Ladies, enough has gone on today. Brya, you need to come home to get some rest."

The two of them were quiet on the ride back to the farm. Brya sat in the backseat staring out at the drizzle. Her body ached and she was reeling from the conversations with Megan and Olivia. When they arrived home, she took more pills, and went to bed. As she drifted off to sleep, she remembered Patch's words, "Take care of yourself and never let your emotion overshadow your reason."

No matter what, Brya would hold fast to that.

The next morning, as the intense sun pried open Brya's eyes, she was still riddled with pain and guilt over her daughter, and surprised that no demons had crept under her door to disturb her sleep. If she could just have been the governor's wife, they would have had everything. Now she had nothing, once again. Not even her daughter.

It was an effort to put on her silk robe and even more of one to slide her feet into her slippers. Her sore hand pulled her hair back and she headed downstairs. James had just come back from the hospital with Megan, and they were seated on the sun porch, talking in low whispers.

"How do you feel?" James asked.

"Not so good," Brya said, slowly pouring herself some coffee. She wasn't quite sure of where to sit, so she opted for the floor, next to a warm window.

"Megan," Brya said, trying hard to ease the strain. "You and James have done so much for me and Olivia. I don't know how to repay you. I could take her back to Santa Fe, but she doesn't want me." Brya took a sip of coffee and continued, "I can remember feeling horribly lost and alone after losing our parents, then again after Holden died. Olivia must be feeling that way now."

Megan wondered where Brya was going with all this. Without any emotion she replied, "I feel that the only way you can repay me is to take Olivia." Megan struggled with this request, knowing that her niece would pay the price.

"After I get dressed, I'll head straight to the hospital to speak with Olivia," Brya said, ignoring her sister. "Maybe I can get through to her before I leave for Santa Fe." She turned to leave.

With this, Megan is aghast. "I can't believe you're not taking her back with you right now!"

"Hear me out, sis, okay?"

"I suppose that it doesn't matter that we're expecting another child?"

This surprised Brya.

"What?"

"You heard me. We need to make room for another youngster, and Olivia needs to live with you. She's your child, for God's sake!"

"Megan, listen to me. She needs to stay here with you until she heals. I want her life to return to normal, as if nothing has ever happened. Everything will turn out fine. You'll see." She got up from the floor, hot and uncomfortable.

"You may lose Olivia if you leave now, Brya. She'll never trust you again to put her first."

Brya could see that James and Megan were furious, but she didn't care. It was her life and she was going to do what she wanted, no matter what they said.

"I give up," Megan said as she stormed out of the room.

James got up from his chair, shaking his head. "Brya, the sooner you leave the better. Megan is pregnant and this arguing isn't good for her." He took his sister-in-law by the shoulders and looked into her eyes, "I hope that the two of you can resolve your differences—after all, you're family."

By the time Brya reached the hospital, it had started to drizzle again. Her stomach ached and she still felt nauseous. It was probably the coffee on an empty stomach, or else nerves. She ordered red roses to be sent to Olivia's room, and before she left, she would buy her some new clothes. Brya knew from experience that those things always perked up a girl.

In Olivia's room, Brya tried to be bright and cheery, but Olivia was lying on her side, staring out at the cloudy sky. This time, she didn't even move her head to acknowledge her mother's presence.

"Olivia, Olivia, it's your mother. Honey, you're gonna be all right. This thing will pass soon, then you'll start to feel better. You are to stay here with Aunt Megan until you heal. I promise that I'll be back then, and when I come here next time, I'll take you with me. You're my one and only wonderful child and we're going to have it all, I just know it! I'm working very hard to find you a father."

Brya talked and talked until she was hoarse. Four dozen red roses arrived from the florist and were placed around the room. A shot of color always brightened things up. But Olivia didn't respond.

Brandon Cole Harrison III

Summer came early to Santa Fe. As the sun came up and Brya slid the curtain back, she watched a mangy, stray dog lick stagnant water from a puddle. Poor thing. He probably had no home. She watched it forage for food on the streets. It walked away slowly, looking for scraps to fill its empty stomach. She would make sure that her daughter would never go hungry like this.

Her daily walk past the plaza held memories of Henry. She hoped that someone else would come along to help her forget.

With Nina's special concealer, the bruises on her face became invisible. But it wasn't that easy to hide the pain in her heart. Her daughter despised her and didn't want to speak to her again. Although Brya telephoned everyday after she left California, Olivia would almost never speak to her. She had locked herself up into some secret world. Brya couldn't reach her yet, but she was determined to find a way.

Brya had become a local, not the exciting young ingenue that everyone wanted. She was twenty-eight and forgotten. But her frightful dreams continued to produce two important ingredients that controlled her waking life: money and family.

Applying cosmetics to the faces of aging screen sirens and porcelain dolls was wearing thin. Even the parties lacked luster with all that incessant talk about the ongoing war.

December 1941 was a bad time for global conflict. On the heels of the Depression came World War II. The Japanese bombed Pearl Harbor and plunged the United States into war. Battles ravaged their way through the steaming jungles of Southeast Asia to the frozen fields of the Soviet Union. Adolf Hitler had built Germany into a powerful war machine, designed to take over the world while Japan and Italy joined forces with him against the United States.

Many young men from New Mexico stationed in the Philippine Islands were killed by the Japanese on the Bataan Peninsula. America's finest were sent to fight never to return. Across the nation, ration coupons were distributed to families for purchase of scarce goods like sugar, gasoline and dairy products. The outcome of World War II was a looming fear for everyone. Brya was no exception, but her own problems were always foremost in her mind.

It was the wiggle in the walk that he remembered. For Brya, it was the obnoxious Texas accent and conspicuous white Stetson hat.

"Well, little lady, I finally found you," he announced, tipping his hat to Brya in the store. His blue eyes danced with mischief and intrigue.

Nina happened to be standing nearby and interrupted. "If it isn't Mr. Brandon Cole Harrison III." She gave him a generous squeeze. "You old rascal. What brings you back to town?"

"Oil, Nina, and lots of it. I'm drillin' a well outside of Santa Fe. Somebody's got to supply this country with gasoline for the war, and it might as well be me." He couldn't stop looking at Brya the entire time.

"Take good care of this gentleman, Brya, he's a real big spender," Nina quipped as she walked away.

"What can I help you with, Mr. Harrison?" Brya asked, nervously adjusting a perfume bottle.

"You can start by joinin' me for dinner tonight," he replied, placing an arm on the counter to get a better look at her turquoise eyes.

She pulled back. Something about him made her jump inside. "I thought you were engaged," Brya blurted out, fidgeting with her bracelet.

He winked at her. "What a great memory you have. Yes, I was, but she's long gone." Cole smiled. "Once I saw you, that was it. How could anyone else compare?"

His power was intense and disturbing.

"I'll pick you up after work about 5:30." This was a deal that he had to close. He had found the one woman that would complement his career.

Brya was left nodding her head as his alligator boots disappeared from sight.

Her heart raced. She ran to the back of the store where Nina was tallying some bills. "Cole certainly has an eye for you," she said, not looking up from her work.

"Nina, tell me about him."

"You could write a book on that one, Brya. Where do you want me to begin?"

"Anywhere, I don't care."

"I heard that he raised more war bonds than anyone to date. He's a self-made oil man, worth millions, who hit one of the largest finds in Texas history. And still a bachelor at fifty-six. Engaged lots of times, but never married."

"I wonder why?" Brya replied.

Nina shook her head. "He never discussed it. His life is a puzzle. With the world at his feet, a man like Cole Harrison is spoiled rotten. He lives in a hotel, has room service and everything else at his fingertips. Why should he have a wife?"

"I'll go to dinner with him, anyway," Brya replied. "What do I have to lose? Besides, this oil man fascinates me."

"Don't flatter yourself kiddo. He's captivated lots of hearts. Like I told you with Henry, tread lightly."

As Brya left to tidy up the store, the words of Mama Beatrice rang in her ears. "When has a little challenge ever stopped you, Brya Fitzgibbons?"

The smell of fresh cilantro, salsa fresca, and carne asada drifted through Epazote, a posh Southwestern restaurant. A mesquite wood fire crackled in a corner of the small room. Cole had requested a table there, for two.

He seated Brya and laid a gift on the table in front of her. Cole was as rugged as a cowboy and as handsome as a movie star. His wavy salt and pepper hair blended into his deep tan.

"For me?" Brya asked sheepishly.

"Who else, darlin'? It's just a little somethin' I thought you'd like. Go ahead, open it."

Brya was hesitant. Fear ripped through her like a sharp knife. Henry had given her presents, too, that meant nothing, only token gestures to lure her into the bedroom.

Cole noticed her hesitation. "Don't be afraid of that little box. It's not goin' to reach up and bite you, for God's sake." He drew out a Cuban cigar and lit it, ordering a Jack Daniels for himself, and one for her, too.

"Could you please put a little water in it for me?" she asked politely.

"Whatever the little lady wants," Cole said, waving the waiter away.

Brya gingerly pulled the grosgrain ribbon off the box and peeked under the white tissue paper. Hosiery, um . . . how personal, she thought, as cigar smoke swirled under her nose, making her sneeze.

"Women always need those things," Cole said. "And since nylons are such a rare commodity during this war, I thought you wouldn't mind owning a couple of pairs."

"My, I've never had such a . . . well, a *special* present from someone before," Brya said, closing the box quickly before the waiter saw the undergarments. Cole was funny. He spoke about nylons like he was discussing racehorses or cattle.

"Glad you like them," Cole replied, proud as punch. He took a sip from his cocktail and watched her. There was something about Brya Hunter that captivated him. She was intelligent, not like the others. Yet her passion was shrouded in a veil of mystery, much like a young queen, trained not to show her feelings. Maybe it was the fact that she had wasted so much time on Henry Buchanan. Cole knew about the affair, having been his campaign manager. But it wasn't important. She would be the one he would marry.

Brya hadn't lost her knack as a clever interviewer. Cole talked on and on about himself: his ranch in Utopia, Texas, where he often entertained presidents of the United States, his six hundred dollar gag gifts to close friends, and the fact that he didn't drive. "I never took the time to learn," he said. "I'd rather haul that old Texas crude out of the ground. Besides, I have Plez, the best chauffeur in the West."

As the fire exhaled its warm breath, Brya became intoxicated by the flamboyant oil and cattle man from Houston, Texas. Thank goodness he didn't ask a lot about Olivia. She wasn't prepared to tell what she had made Megan swear not to talk about. She had to be careful. This, quite possibly, would be her last chance at salvation.

At twenty-eight, Brya's life was topsy-turvy. Conflict was raging on all fronts.

Soon, she would be taking Olivia with her, regardless of what Megan thought. At that point, the relationship with her sister would never be the same.

In six months time, Brya would become Mrs. Brandon Cole Harrison, III. At Cole's insistence, she happily quit her job and moved to Houston. All Brya had to do was get on a plane. He would take care of all the details.

Nina was concerned about her leaving, because no woman had walked down the aisle with this man, and there was more, his proclivity for unconventional sex. To Brya, this didn't matter. He was worth the risk.

At the baggage claim area in Houston, Brya was met by Plez, Cole's longtime companion and Negro chauffeur. He was a handsome black buck about six feet tall, whose pearly white teeth flashed a friendly smile. Brya could tell that he didn't miss a trick. Plez's long, lean torso bent over in a sweeping bow as they met. He graciously escorted her to the back seat of Cole's black Cadillac.

"Well, Miss Brya, Mr. Cole is certainly going to be much happier now that you are here."

Plez had let the cat out of the bag, so to speak, but obviously felt comfortable.

"Will we be headin' to the hotel, Miss Brya?"

"That will be fine, Plez. Thank you." Brya studied the regal chauffeur for a moment. "I can certainly see why Cole has had you for so long."

"Yes um."

Cole was in Washington, D.C., on business. He promised that when he returned, their first night together would be one she wouldn't forget.

He wouldn't either. She was well trained.

This was the lifestyle she wanted and also needed for Olivia. Everything was perfect so far. But she was scared of two things: Olivia and losing Cole.

Plez left her at the door to the hotel lobby saying, "Anything you want done, just ask. I'll take care of it." Cole had rented a suite for Brya at the old El Cortez Hotel where he lived—something that he never did for any of the other women. He wanted her to experience Houston in style. The El Cortez was a stately establishment. White-gloved doormen in gray morning jackets were there to meet her. From her balcony, Houston was big. Everything in Texas seemed to be real big. Even the drawn-out accent had a magnificence about it.

Dozens of scented pink roses permeated Brya's suite. With the Louis XIV furniture, dusty rose chintz fabric, and her newly upholstered daybed, she had the finest money could buy.

Brya stood alone in her new surroundings, missing her daughter. "If only things were different," she said out loud. "At last, I've come home, back to a time before my parents' deaths, when everything was safe and secure."

The telephone rang. It was Cole, back from his trip already.

"How's my sugar pie? I hope that you've been given a royal Texas welcome by the hotel."

"Cole, you've outdone yourself! Where are you?"

"I'm in my suite. Why don't you freshen up and I'll come pick you up at eight. We'll have dinner in."

"In, where?

He chuckled. "In my suite, darlin'. You haven't dined until you've had dinner with Napoleon." He knew she'd rise to the occasion.

Cole's suite was designed for a bachelor, and reeked of stale cigar smoke and alcohol. As Brya first walked in, she felt as though she had entered a sultan's den of iniquity—dark, gaudy, and surreal.

Cole's bedroom held, above his king-sized bed, the biggest surprise of all. Protruding from the wall was a replica of a rocky ledge. Standing with ears pointed low and backwards, poised to jump, stood a life-sized stuffed mountain lion. This sent chills down Brya's spine.

"Meet Napoleon," Cole said, studying her reaction.

"Why did you name him *that*?" she said, shrinking back.

Cole stood there eyeing the animal proudly, his barrel chest puffed out. "Napoleon Bonaparte conquered a lot of territory and so did this fine animal. I have a great deal of respect for the beast."

He walked over and patted Napoleon on the head. "On a huntin' trip at my ranch, I shot the cat in mid-air before it could jump one of my guides. I showed him who was boss, and that's how Napoleon met his demise. He and I go way back, and wherever I go, so does Napoleon."

Brya knew better than to show her dislike for the cat, so she shook one of the claws and politely said, "Nice to meet you, King Napoleon."

Cole grinned. "Why little lady, I admire your spunk."

She stared at the wicked teeth of the predator, a terrifying reminder of what it had once been—a killer.

In one of her mysteries, Brya had read that the cry of a mountain lion sounded like a woman screaming in pain. According to Nina, this was also Cole's trademark. But she would be the one to survive.

Cole offered her a drink as he jingled his double Jack Daniels, enthralled with having everything he needed at the touch of his fingertips.

"Cole, do you plan on us living here in the hotel after we get married?"

"I haven't given it much thought," he replied. "Moving is a big consideration. I warn you that it'll take a lot to convince me to leave here. I wouldn't be able to get room service whenever I needed it. In fact, I wouldn't be able to get a lot of things."

"I understand, honey." She really didn't, but for now, she'd go along with whatever he wanted. Brya knew better than to push the issue.

The evening turned out to be entertaining and imaginative. He told some hunting stories, the best of which was the one about Napoleon, and roared over his 'expeditions' with Plez. He couldn't wait to take Brya to his ranch, and above all, show her off to his friends. The whiskey flowed, the porterhouse steaks were cooked rare, and before Brya knew it, it was late into the evening.

Cole made only one demand. "Be knowledgeable about current affairs. In the circles that I travel in, you will be discussing politics and world affairs at the drop of a hat." That sounded fine. Brya enjoyed stimulating conversation.

After dinner, she lifted her dress and served herself for dessert.

Before she retired to her suite, Cole gave her a plane ticket to California, so that she could share the wedding news with Olivia, in person.

At 6:30 A.M., Brya was startled awake by the telephone. It was Cole, chipper as a song bird.

He didn't even give her time to talk. "Sugar pie, do you think you could manage to throw this wedding by the end of

June? I've reserved the grand ballroom for the evening of the 28th. That's as far as I got."

She rubbed her eyes. It was still a challenge for Brya to think in the wee hours of the morning. "Certainly, sweetheart," she replied in a sleepy voice. "If you give me the names and numbers of our guests, I'll be able to put this together in no time."

"Great. After Plez drops me off at work, he'll be back for you. Come to the office, see Delores, and go over the lists there. By the way, we're entertainin' five hundred guests, never mind the cost. I know you'll do it up right." He hung up.

Brya attempted to hang up the phone but missed the receiver. Five hundred people, in six months?! She'd put together smaller groups for Nina, but this was a different story. However, she would prevail. Cole's phone call woke her up, and she ordered smoked bacon and eggs from room service, and read the newspaper. The war, with its relentless casualties, made her stomach turn. But she would read every newspaper imaginable in order to impress her husband.

After a nice hot bath, she dressed according to Texas standards, which were very high.

⟨⟩

Plez dropped Brya off at Cole's office in downtown Houston. A number of heads turned as she walked through the lobby. Upstairs, she was greeted by Delores, a tall redhead who reminded her of Irene Jones, the woman from whom she and Holden had bought their farm a very long time ago. Dolores had all that high hair, too, green eyes, and a full figure. Must be a Texas thing to have high hair, because not one soul had it in Santa Fe. Those folks wouldn't be caught dead with high hair.

Cole stepped out of his office, "My bride has arrived. Delores, have you given her the lists of wedding details yet?"

"As usual, Mr. Harrison, you're one step ahead of everyone else," Delores replied. "Would you mind if we said hello first?"

Cole glanced at his watch. "Go ahead, you don't have much time."

The two women hurriedly shook hands as Cole escorted Brya inside his office. It was on the top floor of the Houston Petroleum Building, where the view of the skyline was breathtaking. The office was paneled in mahogany, and it had plush red leather chairs and a matching sofa. Brya's daddy's study looked like this, and smelled like it, too. Cole lit up a Cuban cigar and sat down at his desk.

He buzzed Delores. "Where's that wedding list?" he demanded. Poor Delores, he sure kept her hopping.

Delores rushed in with the list. And Brya reminded Cole that the wedding was in capable hands. She got up to leave and kissed him on the cheek, sensing his urgency to get back to work.

"Brya, if you're steerin' the boat, I'm sure we're in for a helluva ride." He never wasted words. "By the way, we're goin' over to some friends' about 8:00. Look pretty."

"I'll be ready, don't worry." Brya winked and sashayed away, utilizing the talent that Cole so admired.

For five months, Brya and Cole indulged in the follies of the rich. This made them a lethal combination. In between wedding plans, they spent many an hour playing card games for high stakes, drinking whiskey, and gambling. It was a good escape for both of them. Under the tutelage of her talented husband, Brya gambled all too easily. She played with a vengeance, cut-throat, like a man.

Racetrack gambling was illegal, but word spread that there were various ranches across New Mexico where heavy betting would take place. Twice, Plez drove the twosome there. No less than a quarter of a million dollars a pop were placed on the horses. And Brya could sit above the track and not sneeze from the smell of hay and alfalfa.

If they were lucky they'd find themselves involved in a floating crap game or slots.

At times, they congregated with friends and played card games such as penuchle, gin rummy, and hearts, hearts being Brya's favorite. The object of the game was not to get any hearts or the queen of spades (black widow), or get as few hearts as possible. Her goal was to run the table where she would receive no points and her opponents would get twenty-five points apiece. Low score won. She was an all or nothing player.

On the flight to California, Brya agonized over Olivia. She wanted her to be part of her wedding day, but that remained to be seen. If only the rape had never happened, she would have had a fighting chance at repairing their relationship.

The plane rattled in the wind, making the landing disturbing and shaky. An unusual cycle of storms had hit the coast of Los Angeles, creating turbulent winds and monstrous waves. Drenched, James, Megan, and Olivia stood at the gate. Rain pelted their umbrellas. It was dusk and the last bit of sun tried to shine through the overcast sky. It threw an ethereal light on all three somber faces.

Brya, outnumbered, swallowed.

"Hello, everyone." She bent down and focused on the vacuous eyes of her child. "Give me a hug, precious."

Olivia slowly put her arms around her mother's neck, giving her an uncertain squeeze. She held her head at an odd, brittle angle like a frightened animal staring into the barrel of a shotgun.

Brya shivered as a few drops of rain trickled down the back of her neck. She pulled her collar higher and stood up. "Hello James, Megan." She stared at her sister's pregnant stomach. "My, look at you, sis. Isn't this wonderful."

"Thank you, Brya," she replied coldly. "Why don't we get out of this crazy weather and head home?"

Brya was not welcome, and she knew it. This time, no colorfully wrapped present could get her daughter's attention. Like a catfish struggling on a tight line, Olivia fought hard to ignore her mother, just as she had been ignored. With any luck, Brya would reel her up to the surface of the perfect world she had created in Houston—family, money, and position.

After her bag was claimed, they dashed through the pouring rain to the car. The radio informed them that the fighting had escalated. Like the Depression, World War II was a cancer. It had spread devastation throughout the world. Although it was not well known at the time, Hitler had started a campaign to murder the Jews, Gypsies, and the Slavs. His dreaded secret police, the Gestapo, arrested anyone they thought was against Nazism. If the war ever reached American shores, Brya never wanted to dive into the trenches and start over like she had in 1929.

Unfortunately, Brya would also have to use coercion and enforced obedience to get Olivia back to Texas. This was going to be a long weekend.

On the ride home, she broke the silence. "I have some great news to share."

Megan rolled her eyes. "What?"

Brya didn't answer. The tension could have been cut with a knife. Olivia silently pushed raindrops around on her slicker. And James, relieved to be home, pulled into the tree-lined drive.

Brya slammed the car door as lightening flashed, illuminating the house. She was overtaken by the pungent smell of blooming citrus. Yes, this had been a nice place for Olivia to stay. But it was time to move on, even though she struggled with what she must do as a mother, and what she thought she was capable of. For Brya, failure was not an option.

The mood was strained. Megan begged off, claiming that her back hurt, and kissed Olivia good night. James followed, having not said two words the entire evening.

Olivia headed toward her ocean paradise in another attempt to avoid her mother.

"Please talk to me, Olivia," Brya pleaded, bending down, taking her by the shoulders.

"About what?" Olivia replied.

"Remember when you were in the hospital, and I said that I would come back for you?"

Olivia nodded. To her, that had been a long time ago.

Brya's eyes flashed their coercive power. "When I leave this time, you're coming with me. You can bring all your favorite things, and the rest will be sent later."

The same frightened animal look came over Olivia's face. "I don't even know you, Mother," she cried. "You're the worst thing that happened to me today."

With deflated courage, Brya pulled her daughter close. Olivia's arms stayed limp at her sides. Brya began to sob. "Please sweetheart, I'm going to make it all up to you. I've met a wonderful man who's going to be your daddy. We're getting married, and he's going to give us everything that I've wished for."

Angry and upset, Olivia jerked herself away from her mother's grip and stormed into the bedroom. She felt so worthless and discarded ever since the Mexican man hurt her—and even more when her mother left. Her world was twisted and distorted. Once she left California, who would she turn to? Who would be her friend?

In a small and distant voice she hollered, "I'll come with you only because I have to. Megan will always be my mommy!"

Brya stood up slowly, reeling from her daughter's words. Suddenly, the faceless ghosts of her stillborn babies floated through her memory. They had been taken from her, but Olivia was her second chance. Brya stayed up all night baking cookies in hopes of appeasing Olivia in the morning.

The weekend was a free-for-all. Cookies were smashed against the kitchen wall. Emotions swept through the house like wildfire. James and Megan were not happy that Brya was marrying, and wanted nothing more to do with her once she took Olivia away from them.

When it was time to leave, Olivia became hysterical and kicked her mother. "Don't take me away, please!" She ran to Megan and threw her arms around her.

Megan knelt down and wiped Olivia's eyes with a handkerchief. Then she took her by the shoulders. "Honey, even though your mommy is taking you, we will always love you. You can count on us, I promise." Fear came over Olivia's face and her body went stiff. Her world as she knew it was being destroyed. She couldn't count on anyone.

The airport was even more chaotic and embarrassing. Brya had to drag her daughter, kicking and screaming, to the plane.

After the rape, Olivia had repressed her feelings and went inward. Undoubtedly, the images of the attackers violating her body were embedded in her memory. What the child had needed most was her mother's comforting arms, not money and phone calls. Now loneliness was the only thing Olivia knew.

Brya felt uneasy as she waited for Plez at the Houston terminal. He was running late—must be the traffic. Olivia stood solemn as a statue next to her mother.

Brya, trying to break the silence, reminisced about Plez, and his tragic history. "Olivia, I want to tell you about Plez, your new father's chauffeur. I think you'll like him."

"He's not my father!" Olivia blurted out.

"Don't be disrespectful. He's the man who's going to make both of our lives better!"

Ignoring her daughter's outburst, Brya continued. "Plez's grandparents were plantation slaves from Louisiana. They died before they saw freedom. Plez said that his parents were a gift to each other during that time, even though they were only poor dirt farmers. He had two brothers and three sisters who worked hard in the wheat fields next to their parents. They cooked and ate what they raised. His mama taught him to be compassionate toward people, and growing up with sisters taught him about women and their needs. He used to be a fireman before he became Cole's chauffeur." Olivia, too young, was more interested in the planes flying overhead.

Just as Brya finished, a black Cadillac came to a screeching halt in front of them. Out jumped Plez.

"I'm sorry to be late, Miss Brya. I had some errands to run for Mr. Cole. He keeps me hoppin' when he's on a business trip."

Plez wiped some sweat from his face and cracked his knuckles while he looked into the deadpan face of Olivia. She hugged her coat against her body and looked down as if someone had beaten her. It was not Plez's place to question, but something was wrong with this child.

"Why, here's the beautiful Olivia that I've been hearin' great things about," he exclaimed.

"Who are you?" she snapped, standing there rigid and cold.

"I'm Plez, the family chauffeur, and I'm here to help you."

"Get away! I don't want you near me!"

Plez, taken aback, muttered 'yes um' under his breath, and quickly left to retrieve the child's baggage. Brya was mortified. What had happened to that sweet and loving little daughter she once knew?

As Brya climbed into the car in silence, her high heels got stuck in the edge of her coat and she almost tripped.

Olivia just looked away with a smirk on her face.

Brya remembered her grandpa telling her that when Olivia grew up, she'd understand. Could that be true?

Plez returned with all of Olivia's suitcases.

"Miss Brya, you're lookin' a little peaked today. Are you comin' down with a touch of that flu that's goin' around?"

"No, Plez, but I've been so on edge about the wedding and other things that I picked up smoking, but don't tell Mr. Harrison." She lit up an unfiltered Camel cigarette.

"This will be our secret, and when you feel the need to light up, just call, and I'll drive you around the block. I'll even buy breath freshener and things to sweeten the air. Mr. Harrison doesn't have to know nothin', Miss Brya. Besides, I has this nervous habit of crackin' my knuckles. Drives everyone batty when they're sittin' next to me, but I can't help it."

"We'll be a fine pair Plez—me puffin' up a storm in the back seat, and you crackin' your knuckles in the front. Hope we don't get fidgety at the same time." Brya laughed nervously and looked at Olivia.

Plez was smart. He observed, listened well, and kept his mouth shut. Cole had one valuable employee.

Meanwhile, the wedding day descended upon Brya. Cole, of course, wanted the best of everything: an evening ceremony, followed by a black tie, formal dinner party for five hundred—a near impossible feat.

Brya intended to surprise Cole and the guests by transforming the grand ballroom of the hotel into the grand ballroom of the French Palace of Versailles—Louis XIV's home. Cole was not to set eyes on it until he walked down the aisle.

The kaleidoscopic colors of crystal and gold chandeliers set the tone of the room. White gardenia and orchid centerpieces fell loosely over gold lamé tablecloths. Rich, woven tapestries imported from France, dressed the walls. A tuxedoed and white-gloved staff added the finishing touch to a six-course seated dinner.

When Brya was a little girl, she would read Mama Beatrice's books and magazines and was always fascinated by the pictures of the palace. Desiring to be a princess and live there, she even memorized the rooms in her head. It was only fitting to recreate it now.

When it was time for the ceremony to begin, Brya made an unforgettable entrance in her champagne satin piece of art, draped to the floor. Her blonde hair fell in tousled curls. The crowd gasped as she slowly paraded by wearing a pearl and diamond necklace from Harry Winston of New York— a gift from Cole. He looked dapper in his tuxedo as they joined hands, bowed their heads, and listened to the minister. When it was time for the ring, the best man handed Cole an eight-carat yellow solitaire diamond. Brya almost fainted. Her ring for him was a single band of gold. Brya didn't believe in a man looking flashy. After the minister pronounced them man and wife, they turned to the crowd. Everyone was smiling but Olivia. Brya had bought her an extraordinary dress in hopes that it would cheer her up. Her daughter reminded her of a cold porcelain figurine, as white as milk and just as vacuous.

Brya's thoughts wandered to the rest of her family, especially her daddy. He would have been so proud. She yearned to have them all there. Eugenia had passed away within the last year, and Patch, heartbroken, died soon thereafter. Brya was unable to give their passing the attention it deserved because of what happened to her and Olivia.

Brock was still working in the oil fields of Venezuela. It was far safer staying there until the war was over. Besides, he was saving a lot of money to come back to Trinity and rebuild the family name again. Emilia contracted tuberculosis after her last concert tour—and the prognosis was not good. She may never realize her dream. Duke enlisted in the army. It was the most noble thing he'd ever done. And James and Megan refused to attend.

The cheering guests jolted Brya back to reality. She gazed out into the crowd one more time, and saw her dear friend Nina. Later, they caught up on a few things. Henry's wife had died within a month of her leaving, and his term as governor was near an end. Brya felt nothing for the man.

As Brya circulated around the room, she realized that her life was now something out of a romance novel. She had been swept up by a knight in shining armor and rescued from a life of shattered dreams. But how would the story unfold? Before the wedding, the problems surrounding Olivia were not discussed with Cole. There was no time and he had too much business to deal with anyway. He proclaimed that at the ranch, the two of them would get to know each other. Olivia was frightened of her stepfather because "he was a man," she said. Tears rimmed Brya's eyes. So far, Olivia had stayed to herself, but later on, there would be no hiding.

She decided to put aside the negative thoughts and get caught up in the gaiety. Nina was plugging her business and would undoubtedly make some good contacts. Just like in the kingly courts of days gone by, the pampered party-goers smoked, drank champagne and gorged themselves on Beluga caviar, shrimp, and Beef Wellington.

The cake was wheeled out, completely draped. After some endearing toasts, it was unveiled to reveal a replica of the Palace of Versailles. Mouths fell open as everyone stared at the masterpiece.

When the last bites of cake were being devoured, Cole leaned over to Brya. "You're the best. You've created a name for yourself here in Houston. No one will ever forget this evening." He nestled in closer and whispered. "Go to your suite and prepare that beautiful body for me. Be at my room by midnight. I have a big surprise for you."

Brya excused herself from the intoxicated company of friends. She only had forty-five short minutes to get ready.

She lifted her full skirt and dashed over to Nina who was to stay with Olivia till morning.

"Cole and I are, well, you know, leaving."

Nina waved her long cigarette holder in the air and raised her eyebrow. "So, it's your bewitching hour, huh?"

"Yes, duty calls." Brya winked at her good friend. "Please make sure Olivia knows where I am and that she goes to bed soon."

"For you, Brya, anything. At midnight, I'll become Aunt Nina."

"You're the best." Brya gave her friend a big squeeze, and ran off, forgetting to say good-bye to her daughter, who was sitting in the corner of the ballroom, alone.

Brya slipped into a luxurious lavender bath and tilted her new ring until it caught the light. As she drizzled warm soapy bubbles down her shoulders, she remembered back to her first wedding night with Holden, who had until now stayed buried in her dreams. His tender kisses and caresses had never been approached by another man. He cared so much for her in his innocent, truthful way. Things had changed, and she was sure that feeling would never be recaptured. But Cole loved her in *his* way.

After every part of her smelled clean and delicious, she slipped on a satin gown and put on a tailored coatdress to disguise her silky undergarments. Her hair fell loosely on the tops of her shoulders, and she wore just enough makeup to accent her eyes and lips. Low satin mules eased her aching feet. She left before midnight.

Cole answered the door quickly, and embraced her gently. In the shadows of the room, someone else was standing. It was another bride!

"Cole, who is this?"

"It's your surprise. Haven't you ever had a ménage à trois before?" he asked.

"A what?"

"It's when three people have sexual relations together. Brya, this will be an experience you'll never forget."

This was too bizarre. "Cole, why aren't we alone tonight?" she pleaded.

"This will spice it up. It will make you feel as if you're making love to yourself, and it will also bring me great pleasure. Do it for your new husband, darlin'."

Brya now understood why Nina had wished her luck with this man. He probably had many perversions, and she supposed this was just her first experience with them. But she knew that in order to keep Cole, she must participate. It certainly wasn't the kind of wedding night that she had envisioned.

He took her hand and introduced her to Doreen, a high-dollar call girl that he bought for the night.

"I wanted a girl that looked like you," he said as he excused himself to get ready, and left the two of them alone together.

Brya didn't think the call girl looked anything like her, even though her figure was exceptional. Besides, what did she have that Brya didn't?

Doreen reached over to softly stroke her face. "I'm only here to make your wedding night more exciting. Would you like some champagne?" she said, gliding over to Cole's bar, pouring two full glasses. Brya timidly took the glass from her hand and stared for a moment.

"Tell me, Doreen, do you do these 'ménage things' often?"

"You'd be surprised at how many men want it. Your husband is no different than a lot of them. He acts out his fantasies, but I know he deeply loves you. Remember, I'm only here as a helper. Take off your dress and stay a while."

Doreen was sweet to try to put Brya at ease in this uncomfortable situation, but Brya had her own method. She decided to drink a lot. Maybe by morning she'd forget what happened.

Doreen playfully flirted with her. "Unzip my wedding gown," she said. Underneath, she wore long, silk stockings and a white garter belt and corset, with her breasts heaving over the top. She sat down in front of Brya, wearing thin, see-through panties, and spread her legs just enough for Brya to see her full, dark hair. Brya became embarrassed, and a funny feeling welled up inside of her, so she gulped another drink.

"Do you like what you see? Do you look like me down there? Show me," she said. She talked in a low, mesmerizing voice.

Doreen knelt down. Brya tried to stop her hands, but then . . .

Doreen softly began rubbing her thighs. "Honey, Cole will want you ready for him when he comes out of the bathroom."

Brya couldn't believe what she was doing. She had journeyed far into another world from which she couldn't escape. Doreen slid her slender fingers inside of her, rubbing gently. She kissed her thighs while she continually stroked her. Brya started to relax. Just then, Cole opened the bathroom door and motioned them to his bedroom. Brya slammed down more champagne. He was ready and climbed on the bed first. Doreen followed, sensuously spreading her legs right next to him. Napoleon's fierce face loomed overhead. Brya was getting drunk and had reached a point of oblivion. They coaxed her onto the bed, kissing and fondling her. Doreen ordered Brya to get on top of Cole. She did, and began moving up and down. Then, after Brya was off of him, Doreen squatted on his face. He held her buttocks cupped in his hands and licked voraciously. In the end, Doreen made sure that when he came, he came inside of his wife.

The next morning, Brya awoke to a spinning room, and Napoleon's face leering overhead. Cole lay next to her, sound asleep. No Doreen. Brya began to cry in her pillow, aware of what she had done. She feared that the man sleeping next to her was a pervert. Cole belonged to the world, and to all women. Her body and hands would never be remembered by him.

But strange as it may seem, she liked it.

Cole woke up refreshed, as if nothing had happened. He rolled over and kissed her as though she were the only woman for him.

"You sure do know how to throw a party. Brya, you're the best thing to come my way in years." Cole pushed her messy hair away from her eyes. "About our honeymoon."

"Yes, Cole."

"I want to take you to Europe, but it's being decimated by the war. When the guns are put to rest and life is back to normal, I'll take you on a splendid trip. I promise."

Brya was not in the mood for talking, even about a honeymoon, so all she managed to do was smile and nod her head, which ached. She needed an aspirin to make it stop hurting.

It was time to go back to her suite and see Olivia. But first, she had one unanswered question that needed clearing up. The best time to discuss business with a man was after sex.

"I'd like to purchase a home with some property, and move there," she blurted out.

"Oddly enough, sugar pie, I'd actually been thinkin' the same thing. It would be far better for your daughter. A hotel is not the place for her. My problem is that I've had complete service for years, and I don't know whether or not I can give up the resort life. Tell you what, I'll make you a deal. I'll give you the money to purchase whatever you want, fix it up, and hire the servants. I'll come for just a short visit. If I like the set-up, I'll stay. If not, I'll head back downtown where I'm comfortable."

"It will be fantastic, I promise." Brya had waited for this chance for years. Finally, she'd have a grand home again, an address to show off, and most importantly, a nice place for her daughter to grow up. Brya felt sure she could persuade him, and even with a headache managed to thank him all over.

Cole added one more thing. "Keep in mind that I want my own suite. It'll make it more exciting when we visit each other, and if we both want privacy, we can have that, too."

"That's fine with me, Cole." In many ways, Brya was relieved. She was not keen on waking up with Napoleon every morning.

Cole escorted her to his front door as if she was just another one of his prostitutes.

There were no tears left. Surely nothing could surprise her now. The marriage and her daughter were filled with uncertainty. Cole was a dynamic individual but they broke the mold when they made him.

Brya decided she could survive this, too. She had made up her mind to look good in public, and swore to make sure her daughter received the best of everything.

As the new bride opened the door to her suite, a dressed and disheveled Olivia was waiting for her. She targeted her mother's eyes. "Where have you been?"

"Where's Nina?" Brya replied, trying to remember if she told Olivia she would be gone for the evening.

Just then, Nina came out of the bedroom. "Boy, am I glad to see you!"

"What's wrong?"

"For starters, you forgot to say good-bye to your daughter at the reception. Then, she refused to get ready for bed and stayed in her dress all night."

Brya crossed her arms over her chest and studied Olivia. Before she could speak, Nina continued.

"As if that wasn't enough, when Olivia saw the Mexican waiter deliver room service, she started screaming. What's going on, here? I thought you had your work cut out for you with Cole, but this one . . ."

Brya waved her hand, dismissing her friend like a servant. No one dared speak badly about her family. "That's enough, Nina. We'll talk later. Thank you very much for watching my daughter."

Brya glared at her defiant child. "You owe Aunt Nina an apology."

Nina grabbed her overnight bag and purse, eager to leave. She spoke quietly and deliberately. "Brya, that was the first and last time you will ever speak to me in that tone. As for your *new* family, I wish you luck."

Olivia never had to apologize.

Legacy

Living in her own world was Olivia's mode of existence. Here, she escaped to great places and talked to imaginary friends who wouldn't hurt her. She painted dark colors on the walls of her hotel room so many times that Cole had to pay to have them cleaned and repainted. Olivia would parade past her mother and Cole in bizarre costumes made from bed sheets. Most of the time, the child wouldn't acknowledge real people, not even her mother. Brya had to make it stop.

Olivia made no attempts to get to know Cole. In one last futile effort, he offered to take her to his ranch in Utopia, Texas, which seemed to arouse some interest in her. However, their first trip wouldn't be until after the New Year.

It was difficult for Brya to balance the demanding sexual needs of her husband and tend to the obligatory urgencies of her daughter. But she was tenacious. Things would work out eventually.

❧

With Cole's money and blessing, it wasn't long before Brya and her daughter were on the doorstep of the distinguished Carrow Hill School. The old gray stone building was set on rolling hills in a prestigious part of Houston.

Miss Howard, the headmistress, reminded Brya of that spindly Miss Grisholm back in Cimarron. She didn't sport any kind of wedding ring.

"How do you do, Mrs. Harrison, and this must be Olivia." She studied them both.

"I'm fine, Miss Howard. Yes, this is Olivia. Say hello to Miss Howard, dear," Brya said, prodding her daughter in the back.

"What did you say your name was?" Olivia said to Miss Howard.

"It's Miss Howard. Now pronounce the name loud and clear," she said as she peered down her nose at the beautiful yet distant child.

Brya left the two of them alone to get acquainted while she wandered around the campus, an old estate of a wealthy financier. A grassy knoll and wooden benches set a warm stage for the young players. Brya felt that Olivia would do well here.

When she returned, Miss Howard looked puzzled and asked to speak with Brya while the child waited outside.

"Olivia is an interesting person, Mrs. Harrison. She's attractive and very bright, but seems a little slow in other ways. I can't put my finger on it. Excuse me for being presumptuous, but is she, well, is she a normal child?"

"What do you mean, Miss Howard?"

"Has she been tested for a learning disorder or hearing problems?"

"No."

"Well, our teachers can test her, if that's all right with you."

"I've never thought of Olivia as having a problem, Miss Howard." Brya had often wondered this herself but would never acknowledge her private fear to anyone. Instead, she flashed her compelling eyes. "If you see any problem that my husband and I should be made aware of, please let us know. But what goes on in this family is our private business—I'm sure you can understand that?"

"Certainly, I do. We'll enjoy having her here and knowing you and Mr. Harrison, as well. She can begin tomorrow."

"Thank you. We'll see you then." Olivia and Brya walked back to the car where Plez had been reading the newspaper.

"Well, now, child," he said as he opened the door, "am I going to be takin' you here to school from now on?"

"I don't want *you* to take me anywhere."

Plez never acknowledged the caustic remarks but he couldn't get used to them, either. Olivia was friendly only when she wanted to be. As for Plez, she treated him miserably.

In one month, Brya found 'Legacy'—a sprawling English Tudor mansion on fifty acres, just outside of Houston. It wasn't as large as the Great House, but it had many similarities. A circular driveway with a high manicured hedge gave the home a tasteful entrance. What took her breath away were two one-hundred foot magnolia trees in the front yard and sunken gardens teeming with roses, peonies, and white-blossomed pear trees.

The home invited relaxation, from the indoor swimming pool to the tennis courts. Large, elegant rooms faced out onto a lagoon, a guest house, and a sizable vegetable garden.

In the solarium, Cole could indulge in his daily habit of sipping morning coffee and reading his newspaper. The upstairs bedrooms had been divided into suites, just as he asked.

Olivia could have friends over for pool parties. There would be plenty of staff to watch them. Their living quarters were located on the property, adjacent to the house. Luckily, 'Legacy' didn't need any remodeling, just redecorating.

Brya began work on the immense project of cleaning up and beautifying her new home. It was early October and she had a huge amount of organizing to do before Christmas. The first order of business was to find a staff and train them, so she solicited Plez's help.

He told Brya that he was confident there were folks that needed a job, and working for the Harrisons would be mighty fine. He'd do some scouting around and be in touch.

"Plez, try to round up people for me by the end of this week. I'll need to get moving on this to make it perfect by Christmas," Brya shouted as he dashed out the door.

Brya found Julie Landau, Houston's top interior designer. They were both antique buffs, and generally agreed on most furnishings. Brya had to be careful to blend her love of French antiques with Cole's rustic, manly look. She chose fabrics of bright yellows, soft earth tones, muted greens, and reds. This way, the beautiful landscape, seen from every room in the house complimented the interior. Cole's suite would have rich mahogany wood and bold fabrics.

Mama Beatrice's daybed, which had been at the El Cortez, would be placed in her suite. It had traveled many miles and was now finally home.

Cole didn't let any grass grow under his feet. He was off raising money for war bonds and drilling more wells. He told his wife to send the bills for 'Legacy' to his secretary, who would pay them with no questions asked.

In one week's time, Plez found several Negroes for Brya to interview, so that she could create her staff to run the house. The first was Cherese, a sweet, young woman, who claimed to be a magnificent cook. She had worked in the kitchens of many wealthy Houstonites. Brya ordered specialty dishes to be brought to the hotel to try, and told her she would then get back to her.

She also needed three maids to clean and take care of house guests. She spoke with several maids at the El Cortez, who had taken care of her. They were eager to leave their hotel jobs and start anew. Brya had gotten to know their temperaments and was confident that they would be committed to do what they did best—cater and clean. In no time, the staff was hired.

Cherese's food turned out to be the best southern cooking Brya had ever tasted—she rivaled Brya's precious Eusabia. She was hired immediately, agreeing not to overdo the butter so that Brya could keep her girlish figure. Lots of fresh vegetables from their garden would be used. Cherese had the sincerity of Eusabia, but wasn't built quite as round.

The only thing missing was the butler. Plez wouldn't do. Brya mentioned it to him, and he just laughed. He didn't want to be inside all the time, and she couldn't blame him. She would interview other men for that position later.

Now she had the staff, the expensive fabrics were ordered, and each day furniture arrived for every room of the house.

The new employees set to scouring and cleaning. Walls were dusted and scrubbed down, while white-suited painters gave the window sills, thresholds and doors a new look. Brya hired a crew to hose down the brick patio areas, clean the clogged rain gutters, and most importantly drain the lagoon. The recirculation pumps were rebuilt and put into operating condition again. The lagoon was stocked with large, Oriental goldfish called 'koi.' The realtor told Brya that the lagoon had been a haven for water moccasins, but there was no cause for alarm as long as they took the precaution to check them regularly.

Renovation was in high gear, and in less than two month's time Brya made 'Legacy' livable—not completed, but clean and presentable enough to bring her daughter and husband.

In addition, she had spent countless hours as a drill sergeant, training the servants in order to make them greatly afraid of her husband. She figured if they were frightened enough, they would do a superb job when he came home. Besides, she had no earthly idea if the man would live here once he saw it, so she couldn't afford to have them make one mistake.

❦

Olivia moved in downstairs, where she had her own small wing, and the two suites upstairs were livable, minus a few choice items such as Napoleon. Brya had a raised platform built behind Cole's bed so that Napoleon could take a prominent position there. She didn't dare move him out of the El Cortez for fear of Cole being angry. The servants knew they were to wait on Mr. Harrison hand and foot.

❦

Cole returned to Houston at a beautiful time of year, Christmas. The better parts of Houston were full of elaborate decorations. To make things picture perfect, a soft, dry snow had fallen, and Legacy was all dressed up in white. Two hand-carved, wooden angels guarded either side of the large oak doors. Over them were red-bowed wreaths filled with miniature gold trumpets, horns, mandolins and drums. Not one thing was out of place.

Plez and Brya greeted Cole at the plane. Olivia had no desire to be there. Instead, she preferred to stay in her room and eat candy bars. Brya indulged, hoping that this would pacify her daughter for the time being.

When Cole hugged his wife, Brya noticed that he looked drained from the flight. He had probably partied far too much.

"Is the house ready?" he inquired.

"Yes, it is, sweetheart," Brya replied, adjusting his turned-up collar.

"Tell me more. Is Olivia finally adapted to being here in Houston?"

"It's all so new to her, Cole. It will take time, but I'm sure you'll be a great influence on her."

Cole ate up the compliment and stood proud as a lion. She was still debating when to tell him about Olivia's rape.

After they settled into the back seat of the Cadillac, Cole pulled out two gifts, one for Brya and one for his step-daughter.

"What is this?"

"Just open the damn thing," he demanded.

When she opened it, she almost cried. There, staring her in the face, was the same kind of corset that Doreen had worn on their wedding night. Part of Brya wanted to throw the thing out of the car window and have thousands of tires run over it, but another part of her wanted to experience Doreen again.

Cole leaned over to Brya and picked up the piece of lacy lingerie, "Wear this for me tonight. I want you."

"Will it just be the two of us?"

"Tonight, yes."

"Then you're in for quite a surprise. Meet me in my suite at nine o'clock sharp," Brya said with a wink.

Cole grinned. "Well, little lady, aren't you somethin'. I graciously accept your invitation."

"Plez," Cole said, "before I see the house I want to stop by the hotel and leave my clothing to be cleaned, then I'll pack an overnight bag to visit Legacy."

Plez nodded in agreement. Brya shot Cole a startled look. "Just an overnight bag?"

"I'll just have to wait and see if I like it," he said curtly.

All that work for nothing, she thought.

Brya took a few deep breaths and tried not to react. They arrived at the hotel, and Cole and Plez disappeared with all of the luggage. He asked Plez to help him pack. Between the two of them, Brya was sure the job wouldn't take long. She stayed in the lobby and purchased a *Time* magazine so she could quickly catch up on world affairs. Boring. She really wanted to people-watch because Houston was interesting that way—so much oil money, jewels, and furs. It was always fun to view the parade.

By the end of 1942, news of the war was better but still disturbing. The Allies finally stopped the Axis advance in northern Africa, the Soviet Union, and the Pacific. Everyone was war-weary. Much of Europe lay in ruins, and millions of people were starving and homeless. When would the fighting end? Brya clutched the magazine to her chest, grateful that Cole had the means to buffer her and Olivia from bread lines and rationing.

When they exited the hotel after forty-five minutes, it had gotten colder outside but the sky was clear, and they could see their breath in the air as they headed toward the car. Driving to Legacy was magical. All the fine Texas mansions were lit up to the hilt. It was like touring a stage production. Cole relaxed, didn't talk much, enjoyed the scenery, and appeared glad to be home.

Brya couldn't tell what Cole was thinking the first time they drove through Legacy's gates. He just sat there, staring at the Old English Tudor, taking it all in. She watched him as he studied the landscape. He asked a few questions here and there until they finally pulled up in front of the brightly decorated entrance. Before there was time to put a key in the lock, the staff opened the door. Brya was so relieved.

They looked spotless in their gray and white uniforms. Cole shook hands with each one, checking them over and over as he proceeded down the line. At the end of the reception, Cherese, bless her heart, held a small tray of hors d'ouvres. Brya hadn't told her to do this. She presented them to Cole, while he examined her a moment, giving her his nod of approval. Shortly, his double Jack Daniels arrived on a silver tray. With a drink in hand, he perused the lower level of the house.

"Where's Olivia?" Cole asked. "I want to give the present to her."

"She's probably looking at the Christmas tree; she was infatuated with it earlier today," Brya replied.

All of the fireplaces were blazing, and their Christmas tree in the solarium looked dazzling. Olivia stood staring at it with her back to them. A window designer from one of the local department stores had collected traditional red and green ornaments and created a tree for Brya. Cole stood on the new terrazzo floor, mesmerized by it all. He glanced up toward the glass-domed ceiling and watched snowflakes fall softly against the glass. Brya thought that, so far, she might have impressed him.

Olivia turned toward her mother, disregarding Cole. "Is this my tree?"

"No darling, this is *our* tree."

"If it was *our* tree, then you would have let me decorate it. Aunt Megan always let me help." Olivia stared at her mother. She viewed her as a small woman in beautiful clothes, but *she* was going to be taller and bigger.

Cole immediately pulled out his present from behind his back. "Olivia, I brought you something special," he said, waving a colorful box in front of her.

Her eyes lit up. "What is it?"

He smiled at her. "I think this is just what the doctor ordered."

In the blink of an eye, the paper was ripped off, and in the box lay her very own ornaments—a pair of miniature pink cowboy boots with twirling silver spurs.

He waved his hand in the air. "Hang those things anywhere on the tree. Whatever makes you happy, young lady."

With enthusiasm, Olivia twirled the spurs and started to place them on a branch.

"Cole, Olivia, *family*," Brya interrupted. "We've already had our tree professionally decorated. Those don't match. We can put the little boots on the tree next year."

Cole was quiet.

With that, Olivia threw her ornaments on the floor and stomped out of the room in tears. Her silence spoke volumes.

Brya felt frustrated, but she had to put her feelings aside to maintain status quo. "I so wanted things to be nice for you, honey. I'm sorry about the outburst."

"So am I." Angered, Cole walked away. He had hoped to establish somewhat of a friendship with Olivia before they left for the ranch. It didn't look like it was going to happen. The child was a complicated puzzle, but so was the relationship between mother and daughter. Why was Olivia so angry? As far as Cole was concerned, no one would move into Legacy without this question being answered.

Brya took Cole's arms and placed them around her neck, kissing him softly on the lips. "Forget this little incident, sweetheart, and pour us another drink. Let me show you your suite. I'll deal with Olivia later."

Brya knew that if she didn't give Cole the night of his life sexually, then the dream of owning Legacy would be over. Yet, she did love him, as crazy as it sounded. They were a perfect match. Her husband was a gamble, but she held an enticing set of cards.

Cole poured them both a stiff Jack Daniels and followed his wife. Brya teased him with the corset as she walked up the steps. But this last altercation with Olivia had somewhat dampened his sexual appetite.

Brya had purchased a king-size bed for him, and on top of it lay a Vicuna throw, a sensual, butterscotch-colored fur. As Cole ran his hand over it, he couldn't help but visually undress his wife. She was such a beautiful creature.

"What's that raised part of the wall with the overhead lights for?" he asked.

"I built Napoleon a podium so he can always be with you." Brya planted a fake smile on her face.

"Why you just thought of it all, didn't you?"

"Anything to please. Wait here, darlin'. I'll be back in a minute."

Brya disappeared into his bathroom and began to draw him a bath. She removed her red cashmere dress and silk slip, revealing her black garter belt and stockings—Cole's favorite. She then removed her bra and replaced it with the corset, admiring the bead work in the mirror. Brya had no intention of taking him to her suite. It was clear that Cole was hooked on the element of surprise. And she intended to take full advantage of that.

While he was away, Brya had acquired a copy of the *Kama Sutra*, the ancient Indian book about the art of love-making. In it, she had learned about new ways to please her lover. In the eighth century, a climax was the closest point to God. She wanted to make Cole feel immortal, even if it was for just one moment.

Brya called her husband in and slowly undressed him. His eyes never stopped traveling the length of her body as he slipped inside the scented, erotic bubbles. She rubbed him all over with tingling mint tree oil until he relaxed and became aroused. His eyes were mesmerized as she did a slow striptease and her lingerie fell to the floor. Anxious to massage him with her strengthened pelvic muscles, she slid in and straddled him.

As the bath water rolled in waves, and the two of them were on the edge of a climax, Cole stopped, holding her tightly on top of him. "Brya, what's wrong with Olivia? Tell me now!" Shocked, Brya stared into the powerful face of her husband. Her chance of living at Legacy was ruined. She began to cry. He shook her. "Tell me!" They locked eyes. Beads of sweat dripped off both of them. He still held his erection and she couldn't move.

"Please don't make me talk. You'll stop loving me."

Cole grabbed her arms tighter. "I said, tell me!"

Tears ran down her face as she remembered that horrible day. "She was raped, Cole," Brya said faintly.

"When?"

She sobbed hysterically. "About a year ago on Megan's farm."

Cole pushed her off and water went flying everywhere. "Why didn't you tell me sooner?"

As she lay against the cold porcelain she felt violated, just like her daughter had. "I wanted the whole thing to go away because I didn't want to lose you." She cried harder. "Please don't make us leave." The hurt and pain of her daddy's death came back to her, and with it, the memory of losing the Great House.

Trembling, Brya dragged her naked body out of the water and went into her suite.

After she dried off, she poured herself a strong drink and curled up on the daybed that had been there for her so many times before. Brya felt like royalty in exile. It was better not to love anyone, she thought, because loving people meant being separated from them, and that hurts. Cole had been brutal and unfair to make her reveal the rape. Had he forgotten that she had lost everyone that she cared for?

Brya refused to leave this palace. Within these walls, she hoped to find happiness and love. She would make sure that Olivia walked the streets with her head held high, proud of who her family was.

❦

The next morning, Brya was up early with the servants. She ached from the inside out. She had spent a tormented and sleepless night. But the house must be brightened up on this dreary winter morning. Brya still had a glimmer of hope.

Of all things, the water pipes had frozen during the night, a rare event in Houston, and there was no water to cook with, or make coffee. The staff was scurrying around hoping to figure out what to do before Cole woke up. Brya had everyone so frightened of him that they couldn't think straight.

Just then, a loud voice boomed down from the top of the stairs, "If there's no water, then fill up some pans with snow and melt the damn stuff on the stove!" There stood her husband, bare-chested, with his robe flying open, shouting orders. From that moment on, Legacy became his.

Now that Cole knew the truth, he was certain that he could work things out with his new family.

He telephoned the El Cortez and requested that Napoleon be brought to his new place of honor. After thirty years in residence, Cole Harrison gave up his suite.

Brya was numb. Tears of joy ran down her face. She walked out onto the front porch of her new home to get a breath of fresh air. With her life beginning again, there would be no room for nightmares and no use for pills. Finally, she was able to take the residue of her past, scrape it off her feet, and move on. On either side of her, standing tall and strong, were the two hand-carved angels. Overwhelmed, she patted herself on the shoulder and looked up to the sky.

"Eusabia, I do have my guardian angels with me. I'm living grand again with my very own family, and I will never, ever leave them, no matter what."